GILL LOBEL

Forever Family

W

ORCHARD BOOKS

Pearl was running across a buttercup meadow. Quick, quick – she was almost there!

So near you could touch it – there, right there, where the tree tops brushed the clouds – a huge rainbow arched into the sky. Pearl stretched out her hands to catch the rainbow before it disappeared.

Way ahead, a figure floated up into the rainbow, bathed in swirls of red and orange, of yellow, and green and violet and blue. She bent down and seized Pearl's hand, and then she was up, up, flying through ribbons of light. Higher and higher she went, then the figure turned towards her and smiled, and Pearl saw that it was Mum. Pearl laughed with joy as they twirled and danced in a kaleidoscope of colour, until they reached the top of the rainbow.

'Now here's the fun bit,' said Mum. And throwing back her head and laughing, she whooshed down the rainbow.

'Come and catch me!' she cried.

Pearl started to slide after her, but the rainbow seemed to be melting.

Dark clouds swirled around her.

'Mum – Mum, where are you?' she shouted. 'I can't see you!'

Lightning flashed and thunder roared.

'Don't leave me, Mum, don't leave me!'

Chapter 1

Pearl sat bolt upright in bed, her heart pounding, her hands wet with sweat.

'All right Pearl, I'm here, I'm here.' Jenny stumbled sleepily into Pearl's room.

'Was it a bad dream, Pearl?'

Pearl nodded. She tried to speak, but her breath came too fast.

Can you tell me about it, love?

Pearl shook her head. There were some things you just couldn't talk about—

Jenny got her a drink of water and plumped up her pillow. She sat on the edge of the bed, and patted Pearl's hand until her breathing slowed, and she went to sleep.

In the morning the dream was still there, and Pearl couldn't get it out of her mind.

'Come on chick – pop your shoes on, Bernie will be here in a moment.'

Moodily Pearl poked the carpet with her toe. 'Do I have to go?'

'Oh Pearl – just give it a try!' Jenny put her arm around Pearl. 'You never know – you might enjoy it!'

Through the window, Pearl saw Bernie's little red car pull into the drive. Bernie waved to her as she got out. Pearl turned away. Bernie was all right – as social workers go – but why did she keep making her do things she didn't want to?

'Hi Pearl! Wow, you look terrific!' Bernie breezed into the room, smiling brightly.

Slowly Pearl raised her eyes until she was looking straight into Bernie's. 'I'll go – just this time – but I'm not staying over' She pressed her lips together stubbornly.

'You don't have to stay over, love,' said Bernie gently. 'Just go for tea, and see how you get on. Kathy and Jamal are really looking forward to having you.'

Kathy and Jamal. Pearl remembered when she had first met them. Jamal was all right, but Kathy kept making a fuss of her, and she didn't like that.

And then there had been all that talk about a 'Forever Family'.

'I'll just go for tea,' said Pearl firmly. 'But I'm not staying there – ever – and I don't want any stupid *Forever Family*. I want to stay with Jenny until Mum's better.'

'I see.' Bernie sighed and shook her head at Jenny. 'Come on, then, love, let's get going.'

8

It was a long drive. Pearl watched the rain trickling down the car window, while Bernie rabbited on about how wonderful Kathy and Jamal's house was. Bernie did go on sometimes!

'And they've got a cat and a guinea pig, Pearl. And a big garden with an apple tree, and a swing—'

Pearl began to draw in the mist on the window pane. She drew a little canal boat. At the window were her bluebird curtains, and on the roof a row of plant pots, full of flowers. Then she drew a tree overhanging the boat, a golden blossom tree that smelled of sweetness and summer.

'And I think there's a climbing frame in the garden, too,' concluded Bernie.

Pearl sniffed. Really – anyone would think she was a little kid!

Bernie turned the car into a wide driveway.

The front door opened, and there was Kathy, all smiles, and Jamal behind her.

'Hi, Pearl – we're so glad to see you!'

Pearl hoped very much that Kathy wasn't going to kiss her. She followed Jamal into a big room. There was a real fire burning in the grate, and the table was set for tea.

Pearl stared hard at the carpet.

'Would you like to see the guinea pig?' Kathy held out her hand.

Pearl did not take it. Why did everyone treat her like

9

a baby? Was it because she was small for her age? It was infuriating!

Jamal took her out the back. It was true – there was an apple tree, and a climbing frame, and a cat and a guinea pig.

The cat was a big ginger tom, with green eyes. Pearl thought about Tiggy, about the soft feel of her tortoiseshell coat, and how they used to rub heads first thing in the morning. She had to blink her eyes hard so she didn't cry.

After she had fed the guinea pig, Kathy said it was time for tea.

'Where's Bernie?' asked Pearl.

'Oh – she's just popped out to do a bit of shopping,' said Jamal cheerfully. 'She's coming back to get you about seven.'

There were sausage rolls and mini pizzas, and little sandwiches cut into animal shapes. There was coke, and jam tarts and chocolate cake. *Baby stuff,* thought Pearl scornfully.

She did her best to eat, but the food kept sticking halfway down.

'Aren't you feeling well, Pearl?' Kathy put her arm round Pearl's shoulders. 'You don't have to eat if you don't want to.'

Pearl wriggled away furiously. She felt her eyes sting and her nose began to prickle.

'I – want – to – go – home!' she gasped.

'I'll phone Bernie,' said Jamal. 'It's all right, Pearl, we'll ask Bernie to take you back to Jenny's house early. Don't cry, love.'

'I'm not crying!' shouted Pearl. 'I want to go really home – not Jenny's house – my own home on the boat. I want my own, real mum! And I want Tiggy back, too!'

'Oh dear,' said Kathy. She looked helplessly at Jamal.

'Pearl, you can't go home,' said Jamal gently. 'Your mum's not well enough to look after you anymore.'

'Yes she is!' shouted Pearl. 'She just needs me to go home and make her better. Why won't anyone let me go home!'

That night, after Jenny had kissed her goodnight, Pearl got out of bed, and opened her wardrobe door. Right at the back of the wardrobe, underneath a heap of shoes, was a cardboard box. Pearl reached inside, and drew out a book. On the cover was an apple tree by moonlight. She turned to page sixty-four.

Whenever the moon and stars are set,
Whenever the wind is high,
All night long in the dark and wet,
A man goes riding by.

Late in the night when the fires are out,
Why does he gallop and gallop about?

She whispered the words softly to herself.

That was a poem she and Mum loved especially.

She turned to the front of the book, and stroked the writing on the inside page. It said:

> To Pearl, my treasure,
> with all my love,
> Mummy
> xxxx

Then she hid the book carefully in its cardboard box, and climbed into bed.

She twisted her hair tightly round her finger. She closed her eyes, and went inside her head. Then she was back on the canal. Underneath her the boat rocked gently. In the next room, Mum was playing the guitar, and singing, and through the open window drifted the sweet scent of elderflowers.

Chapter 2

'Mrs Parsons, tell Pearl Lovett to move – she's sitting in my place!'

'No, she's not, Amy; I'm afraid I've moved you – to the table in front of my desk. Perhaps that way you'll get some work done today!'

Amy Perkins scowled and gave Pearl's chair a sly kick as she dragged her bag over to a single table right underneath Mrs Parson's nose. 'Just you wait till break!' she hissed.

'I heard that, Amy,' said Mrs Parsons. 'See *me* at break! Right, Pearl dear, can you come out to the front please? I'm looking for someone with a good, clear voice, to do the reading in assembly tomorrow.'

Pearl flushed with pride, and opened the book Mrs Parsons gave her. She read aloud, nice and clearly, and with lots of expression, the way Mum had taught her.

A snigger came from the front table.

'And I heard that too, Amy Perkins,' said Mrs Parsons. 'It's a pity more people in this class don't read as beautifully as Pearl.'

Now she'll really do me at dinner-time, thought Pearl. *Why – why, why, why do I have to come to this horrible place every day?*

As she read, her mind drifted back to the cosy mornings back on the boat. After they'd washed up the breakfast things, she and Mum would read together over a cup of hot chocolate. Then they would go outside and run along the canal tow path, in the freshness of the morning, and feed the ducks, and laugh and joke. And most mornings they did some painting. Mum would take her sketch pad outside, and while she drew, Pearl painted whatever she saw – boats and dragonflies, ducks and flowers...

'...that was excellent, Pearl – you're just the person I was looking for!'

Pearl came to with a start. Mrs Parsons was smiling broadly at her.

'Right, off you go, dear – and you can choose a new book from the book box, if you want to.'

Pearl went over to the book corner. She felt a bit scared at the thought of reading aloud in assembly, but proud, too. She rummaged happily through the book box.

That was the best moment – choosing a new book. She picked out a story about a girl who lived in America long ago, and took it back to her table.

Grace Joseph gave her a little smile.

'Don't take any notice of that Amy Perkins,' she whispered. 'She can't read for toffee!'

Pearl flashed her a grateful smile, and lost herself deep in the wild woods of America. When the bell went for break, she took the book outside with her – it was getting really interesting; Sarah and Jane were all alone in their log cabin, while outside a pack of wolves howled eerily in the moonlight. Perhaps she could find a corner where she could read in peace and quiet. She wandered off towards the wildlife garden, and curled up on a bench. There was a little pond there, and sometimes, if you were lucky, dragonflies.

'Hi, Pearl!' It was Grace, smiling broadly. She was holding a copy of *Pop Stars Weekly.* 'Who's your fave pop-star?'

Pearl smiled. 'Chanterelle, of course!'

'Mine too!' shouted Grace.

They sat side by side on the bench, sharing the magazine. There was an interview with Chanterelle, and then they did their stars with Mystic Mae.

Grace was Aquarius.

'Your lucky day is Sunday,' read Pearl, 'and you love shopping. Look out on Wednesday, and your best friend will tell you an amazing secret!'

'What star sign are you, Pearl?' asked Grace.

'Pisces,' said Pearl shyly.

15

'Let me do yours now!' Grace grabbed the magazine. '"Your lucky day is Tuesday, and you love animals. Your star day is Friday, when a funny friend will make you smile." Hey – it's Friday today! Would you like to see my famous Chanterelle impersonation?'

'Go on then,' said Pearl.

Grace leaped to her feet, clutched an imaginary microphone to her mouth, and turned her back on Pearl. Singing throatily, she wiggled her bottom so furiously, that a little group of giggling girls gathered round to watch. Grace's performance got so dramatic that three dinner ladies came over to see what was going on.

For a few moments Grace wiggled and sang, oblivious of the crowd behind her. Then she turned round, put her hand over her mouth, and collapsed into an embarrassed heap beside Pearl.

'That was cool, Grace, really cool!' Pearl gasped with laughter, as everyone – including the dinner ladies – burst into loud applause.

Pearl hadn't had so much fun in a long time. The bell went for the end of break, and Grace grabbed her hand as they ran off back to the classroom. She had made a friend!

Grace even looked a bit like her. The children at her last school, Norton Green, had all been white. It felt good to have a friend who looked like her – only while Grace's hair was black and tightly curling, hers was a sort of dark gold, and she had Mum's green eyes.

16

When Pearl was very little she had sometimes wished she had pink rosy cheeks and copper-gold hair like her mother; but Mum always said she was beautiful just as she was.

They used to play a little game; Mum would say, 'Who's my treasure?'

And Pearl would say, 'I am!'

'And who's my beautiful daughter?'

Then Pearl would shout, 'ME!'

And Mum would tickle and tickle her until they were both breathless with laughter.

After break it was maths. Pearl found herself struggling. Mum didn't like maths very much, so they didn't do it very often. She got horribly stuck, but then Mrs Parsons came over to her table, and helped her.

The last lesson in the morning was art. Pearl cheered up – art was her very best thing.

'Right, everybody,' said Mrs Parsons. 'We're carrying on with patterns this morning. I want you to design a pattern using wildlife as a theme. You can use paints, charcoal, crayons – anything you want.'

Pearl couldn't wait to begin. She knew exactly what she was going to do. She dipped her brush into the red paint. Then carefully, carefully, she outlined one of the beautiful roses that Mum used to paint on the trays and plates she sold at craft fairs.

She knew just how to do them. First she did the red rose, and then the white. Then she painted three green leaves around each rose, and highlighted them with little strokes of yellow. When the paint had dried she added tiny yellow dots for the stamens in the centre of the roses. She mixed a deep pink and very gently shaded the white rose.

They looked so fresh, so real, she could almost smell them.

'Wow, Pearl, that's really wicked!' Tom Baker leaned over to admire her painting.

'Yeah – pity she can't add up though.' Amy Perkins paused on her way to show her work to Mrs Parsons. 'What's two plus two, Pearl? Or is that too hard for you?'

'Don't take any notice, Pearl,' said Grace, 'she's just jealous!'

Mrs Parsons was far too sensible to admire Pearl's work. But she gave her a warm smile as they packed away before the bell.

Pearl had enjoyed the art lesson so much, she had forgotten Amy Perkins' threats. But it was all right anyway, because Grace stuck to her like glue throughout dinner time, and so apart from a few insults, Amy couldn't do anything.

Pearl really dreaded school dinners. As soon as she saw her plate of greasy fish fingers and soggy chips, her appetite vanished, and she just couldn't eat it. Pudding was much better – chocolate rice-crispy cakes. She managed to eat one.

Suddenly the day seemed far too long, and she longed to be on her own. It was hard being with so many people all day. Mostly Mum had taught her at home, but sometimes, when they docked at Norton Green, she had gone to the village school.

That hadn't worked out, though. Some of the children made nasty remarks about her clothes. And they called her rude names, too; Gypo, and once, stinky pants. That wasn't true – Mum washed all their clothes carefully – but it was hard to iron things on a canal boat, and anyway, Mum said life was too short for ironing. Then there was the time when two boys trapped her behind the dustbins. The big boy with the runny nose pushed her against the wall and laughed when she bumped her head. He called her chocolate drop, and then the little skinny one called her something much worse, and she hit him hard and ran all the way home, sobbing with rage.

After that Mum had kept her off school, and taught her at home. Sometimes Pearl thought it would be nice to have other children to play with, but here, at Willowbrook, there were so many. Pearl felt dizzy with the dozens of faces that swirled around her all day.

After lunch it was music, and then library till home time. Pearl collapsed with relief into the warmth and peace of the library. She chose a book all about dolphins and found a table on her own, in a quiet corner. Soon she was swimming in a warm blue sea, surrounded by dolphins. She twirled and dived as the dolphins glided around her, calling to her with their strange high-pitched cries. They came close and let her stroke them. She placed her arm on a blue fin and the dolphin smiled and drew her through the water. Silver bubbles streamed all around her.

'Right, if you want to take out a library book, make your way quietly to my table to have it stamped.'

It was Mrs Jackson, the librarian. Pearl jolted awake. A queue had formed in front of Mrs Jackson's table.

Pearl looked around carefully. No one could see her. Very quickly, she slipped the dolphin book into her bag.

That night, before she went to sleep, Pearl took the book out of her bag. She turned to the inside page. Very neatly, in her best handwriting, she wrote:

To Pearl, my treasure,
with all my love,
Mum

xxx

For a moment panic and guilt swept over her. Then she stroked the words slowly and lovingly. It was all right. Mum would have wanted her to have such a lovely book.

Chapter 3

From the pages of a big scrap book a face beamed up at Pearl. *It's me*, she thought. *Little Pearl.*

Little Pearl was wearing a bright red top and navy leggings. Embroidered on the top was a tiny rainbow.

Mum had done that. She loved rainbows. She painted them on the glasses she sold at craft fairs. She painted them all over the boat. And she embroidered them on Pearl's clothes.

My rainbow clothes, thought Pearl. *Rainbow days.*

'Penny for them?' said Bernie.

Pearl sighed. 'I was just thinking…about when I was little…'

Bernie nodded. 'That's a lovely photo of you, Pearl. I suppose you must have been about two, then.'

Pearl turned the page.

There was the boat, bright with new paint, with the little castles and roses Mum had painted all over her. And there,

21

right in the middle, next to the words THE ELDERFLOWER, picked out in black and gold lettering, was a little painted tree hung with creamy blossoms, all fresh and alive.

A magic tree.

Her boat. Her tree.

'Tell me about the boat,' coaxed Bernie.

Pearl opened her mouth to speak, but suddenly there was a hard lump in her throat, and she couldn't talk.

'OK, sweetheart, not if you don't want to,' said Bernie softly.

She waited for a while, until Pearl began to turn the pages again.

Her Life Story book.

Her whole life.

After the dreadful night when social workers carried Pearl, kicking and screaming out of Mum's arms, and out of the only life she had ever known, they had made a book for her. They filled it with all the photos of Pearl and her mum they had been able to find on the boat.

There was Tiggy curled up on a crocheted blanket, fast asleep by the stove.

There was her fifth birthday party, before Mum started to get ill. Pearl was blowing out the candles on a ballerina birthday cake. She was wearing a lilac dress with silver stars scattered all over it, and little matching shoes.

Pearl remembered how Mum had kept the cake as a surprise. How had Mum managed to bake it without her knowing? She traced her fingers over the photograph, feeling the silky white icing, the sugar-pink scallops on the skirt of the cake, and the little smiling ballerina in the middle. She had loved the cake so much, it seemed a shame to eat it. And however had Mum got the little ballerina right in the centre of the cake like that?

And there was Nanna. Pearl swallowed hard.

Nothing had been the same after Nanna died. That was when Mum had first started to get ill.

When she started to stay later and later in bed.

When she wouldn't eat, and Pearl had to coax her with Marmite on toast.

When she started bringing home lots of cans from the village shop.

Then for a time she would laugh again, and they would have wonderful fun, and Mum would giggle like a girl, and whirl her round the boat until she was dizzy. But then Mum would sleep and sleep, and not get up. And when she did get up, she was very sick, and Pearl used to bring her water to rinse out her mouth, and make her a cup of tea.

Pearl turned another page.

And there was her best photo, the one of her and Mum together, the day Tiggy came. Tiggy was in *her* arms – oh, so sweet, and little and fluffy, and Mum had *her* arm right round both of them. That had been a good day. Mum hadn't been sad at all, and they had a special welcome party for Tiggy, with a little kitten cake made from white

23

fish, and coke and crisps for her and Mum. They made Tiggy her very own warm bed out of a cardboard box, lined with an old fluffy cardigan, and Mum had knitted her a tiny toy mouse. On the outside of the box Pearl had painted an under-the-sea picture, with shells, and brightly coloured fish, and waving seaweed. A little mermaid peeped shyly out of her shell palace. Mum said it was the best thing she had ever done.

'That's a beautiful photo, Pearl,' said Bernie. 'Can you tell me a bit about it?'

Pearl shook her head silently.

How could she tell Bernie about something so special – so special that it hurt to even think about it?

Bernie turned the page.

There was Pearl, standing straight and stiff, next to Jenny.

Over the page was a photo of her with Kathy and Jamal. Kathy had her arm round her, and Pearl was pulling away ever so slightly. Kathy and Jamal were smiling, but Pearl had her face turned away from the camera.

'You know that day, when I picked you up from Kathy and Jamal's house?' said Bernie. 'Can you tell me what went wrong?'

Pearl bit her fingernails hard.

'Don't you like Kathy and Jamal?'

Pearl sighed deeply. 'It's not Kathy and Jamal. They're all right, I suppose. But I've told you, *I don't want a Forever*

Family. I'll stay with Jenny for a bit until Mum's better, and then I'll go home. Mum *needs* me. She'll get ill again if I don't look after her. And what about Tiggy? I miss her so much!'

'Pearl, sweetheart, Mum's much too ill to look after you at the moment. She'll need to stay in hospital for a long time. It may be, Pearl, that your mum won't ever be able to look after you properly. That's why we need to find a family where you can stay till you're grown-up – a Forever Family. And if Mum gets a lot better, you'll be able to see her sometimes. You can write to her now, you know.'

Pearl felt as if her heart had stopped beating.

Not to go back home – perhaps never?

She felt her throat tighten. Tears filled her eyes. She blinked them away furiously.

She would not cry!

But the tears would not go away, no matter how hard she screwed up her eyes.

Hard sobs shook her through and through.

Slowly she rocked backwards and forwards on the sofa. She cried and cried till she had no more tears left, and then she buried her face under a cushion.

Bernie patted her on the back awkwardly.

And then Pearl found her voice. 'I want my mum,' she sobbed, 'I want my *own* mum – not you, or Jenny, or anyone else!'

She picked up the Story of her Life, and hurled it across the room.

4, Cherry Tree Close,

Granby

Buckminster

BS5 4ND

Dear Mum,

How are you? Are you feeling better? Bernie said I could write to you. Is it all right at the hospital? I'm all right. Jenny is OK and so is Bernie, but they keep going on about a Forever Family. And I don't want that Mum, I want to go back home with you to the boat. There's these people, Kathy and Jamal, right, and they want to adopt me. So please, please get better quickly, Mum, before they take me away from you forever. I miss you so much, and I'm scared they won't ever let me come back to you.

I told them I would look after you if they let you come home, but they don't listen to me. Bernie, she's my social worker, she says they found Tiggy a good home, which is silly because she already had a good home, only they smashed it up. I can't help crying Mum, when I think of Tiggy. When you're better we'll go and get her back shall we?

26

Please keep taking all your tablets, Mum, and get better soon! I've drawn you a picture of us all on the boat, so you won't forget. And we've been doing these word and shape poems at school. I've done a special one for you. (You have to read it downwards first.)

Love you lots and lots,
Pearl

xxxxxxx

P. S. Please, PLEASE write back soon! I look in the post every day, but I haven't had a letter from you yet, so I guess maybe they don't let you write at the hospital?

This is the poem.

M eans all the world to me
O nly one for ever
T akes care of me
H olds me safe
E mpty is the world without you
R ing of love around me

Chapter 4

'Don't forget your swimsuit, Pearl!'

'I won't!'

Pearl jammed her towel into her sports bag. As if she would forget!

She ran all the way to school, her heart singing. Ever since she posted that letter to Mum, she had felt so much better. It was almost like talking to her, and Bernie had said that if Mum made good progress, they would arrange for Pearl to visit her at the hospital. She was sure that as soon as Mum read the letter, she would see how important it was to get better quickly, so they could be together again.

And today she was going to tea with Grace Joseph.

And it was swimming!

After art and library, Pearl's favourite lesson was swimming. Willowbrook children were lucky – they had their own little pool, so everyone had a chance to learn to swim.

But Pearl didn't need lessons; one thing Mum had been very strict about was safety on the boat. When she was very little she always had to wear her life jacket whenever she was up on deck, and right from babyhood, Mum had taught her to swim. Sometimes they went to the swimming baths, but often, in the summer, they paddled about with the ducks. Some people said it wasn't safe to swim in the canal, but Mum said so long as she was with her, it was all right.

Pearl fidgeted impatiently all through maths, slipping her hand into her swimming bag, to feel the cool silk of her costume. It was green and blue, with little sparkly whirls. Jenny said she looked like a mermaid in it.

At last Mrs Parsons said the magic words.

'Right everyone, pack away quietly – I said *quietly* Jamie Kershaw – and line up in silence by the door.'

It was hard to walk down the corridors 'in an orderly fashion', as Mrs Parsons ordered. Pearl's legs longed to run and jump.

She couldn't help breaking into a run for the last few metres.

'Oh Pearl, I love your swimsuit!' Grace pirouetted around the changing rooms.

'All right if you like all that glitter.' Amy Perkins wrinkled her nose.

'Ignore her, Pearl,' advised Grace. 'She's only jealous.'

Amy sniffed loudly, and looked at Pearl as if there was a very bad smell under her nose.

'Why on earth would I be jealous of *her*? Her own mother doesn't even want her!' Amy flounced off to the pool.

Pearl felt a surge of rage flow through her. She sprang after Amy, her fists clenched.

'Pearl, stop!' Grace grabbed her arm and pulled her back. 'Don't hit her, Pearl. If you do that, then *you'll* be the one gets into trouble! She'd really love that!'

Pearl collapsed onto a bench. Tears filled her eyes, hot and strong. She was shaking all over.

'It's not true, what she says, Grace – Mum does want me, only she's ill, see…and I've written to her, and told her to hurry up and get better, and soon as she can she'll come and get me, I know she will!'

"Course she will, Pearl.' Grace squeezed her hand gently.

'Why does Amy hate me so, Grace? What have I ever done to her?' Pearl rubbed her nose quickly with the back of her hand.

'She's jealous, Pearl – because you're much cleverer than her – and because I used to be her best friend.'

'You were Amy Perkins' best friend?'

Grace nodded.

'When I first came to Willowbrook, from Birmingham, she was real nice to me. She always hung around with me at break, and she didn't laugh like the other kids – because I spoke funny – you know. And she never called me names – about my colour, like some of the others. But when I got to know her better, right, I found out she was really spiteful. She'd say one thing to your face, and then go and talk about you behind your back. That's why she had no friends.'

'I never knew you had a bad time when you came to Willowbrook,' Pearl whispered.

'Yeah…but you soon learn who the really nice people are…and Mrs Parsons really did Amy for what she said about me. And now you're my best friend, Pearl, and that's *another* thing she hates you for.'

Pearl's heart missed a beat. 'Am I really your best friend, Grace?' she asked shyly.

'Course you are, you banana. Why do you think you're coming to my house for tea tonight!'

Pearl stood up straight and tall. She felt warm all over.

'Come on – last one in the water's a dead duck!' Grace dashed off laughing to the pool.

It was a brilliant swimming lesson. Pearl was put in the top group, with the really confident swimmers. She learned how to dive properly, and worked on her front crawl. Then for the last five minutes they were allowed free play.

She and Grace, and a shy girl called Marina pretended to be dolphins, and twisted and twirled together. Then they tried underwater swimming to see who could hold her breath longest.

When the whistle went, Pearl felt relaxed and happy. *I like it here,* she thought, *I really like it here. And now I've got a best friend, too!*

31

Science passed in a haze.

'I think we've lost you, today, Pearl,' said Mrs Parsons, when Pearl mislaid her work sheet for the third time. 'You're off with the fairies this morning!'

'Sorry, Mrs Parsons.' Pearl blushed.

It was true; her head was in a whirl of excitement.

She'd got a friend – a special friend.

For the first time Pearl realised that she had sometimes been lonely on the boat. Sometimes – just sometimes – it would have been nice to have someone of her own age to go around with.

And she was going to tea with Grace.

As home time drew nearer, Pearl curled up in a quiet corner of the library. She had found a beautiful book of verse for children. It was brand new and glossy. Stunning pictures glowed from every page; and yes, there was one of her very favourite poems.

Softly she whispered the words to herself:

> *The tide in the river,*
> *The tide in the river,*
> *The tide in the river runs deep.*
> *I saw a shiver*
> *Pass over the river*
> *As the tide turned in its sleep.*

A delicious shudder ran down Pearl's back, and the hair on her head tingled.

'Time to get your books stamped, everyone!'

Mrs Jackson's voice, far away at the other side of the library, snapped Pearl out of her dreams.

She held the book to her face and sniffed its lovely, fresh, new book smell.

Mum would really love me to have a book like this, she thought. *She would buy this for me if she could.*

She went to slip the book into her bag.

Suddenly her hand froze.

Was what she was doing wrong?

It wasn't *stealing*, was it?

When Mum's better, she'll come to school and pay for the books, thought Pearl.

All of them.

Because there were at least six books now in the cardboard box in the wardrobe.

Very quickly, before she had time to think any more troublesome thoughts, Pearl stuffed the book into her bag.

And at that exact moment, Amy Perkins turned into Pearl's little bay to return a book.

Her eyes shot open.

'Oooh – er!' she said.

Pearl's heart jumped wildly.

A black tide flowed in front of her eyes.

33

There was Mrs Jackson, looking down at Pearl.

And her eyes were hard and unsmiling.

Pearl felt a rush of blood to her face.

'I'll have that book, thank you,' said Mrs Jackson. 'Have you ever done this before, Pearl? Because we've had quite a few books go missing lately.'

Pearl tried to speak, but her mouth had gone dry.

'I think you and I had better go and have a word with Mrs Wells, Pearl.'

Her face buried in her hands, Pearl followed Mrs Jackson out of the room. Out of the corner of her eye, she saw Grace's astonished face, and the smile of triumph on Amy Perkins'.

The half an hour Pearl spent with the head teacher was one of the most uncomfortable times in her life. But Mrs Wells didn't shout at her. She put her arm round Pearl's shoulders, and gave her a paper hanky for her nose.

And Pearl found herself pouring out all her grief and sorrow. She told Mrs Wells everything – about how she missed her mum, about how she wanted to go back to her own home, about missing Tiggy. And about the books.

'Mum would have paid you for the books, Mrs Wells,' croaked Pearl.

'I'm sure she would, dear.' Mrs Wells gave Pearl another paper hanky. 'But it was wrong to take the books, Pearl, you know that really, don't you? It's stealing, isn't it?'

Pearl nodded.

'I'm sorry, Mrs Wells, I'm really sorry,' she choked.

Then Mrs Wells made Pearl a cup of hot chocolate in her special flower mug, and let her wash her face in her own little cloakroom.

'Now, I'm afraid I shall need to send a letter home, Pearl,' said Mrs Wells. 'Jenny will need to know what you've been doing – and how you feel about everything too, dear. And of course, you must bring the other books back.'

Pearl nodded speechlessly.

A letter home! Whatever would Jenny think of her?

She would be so disappointed in her. Would she say she didn't want Pearl anymore?

Perhaps she would write and tell Mum!

Perhaps Pearl would be sent to a Children's Home.

When the bell went, Mrs Wells sent her back to her classroom. Pearl hung around for a while, hoping all the other children had gone home.

How could she face anyone again? And what would Grace think? Now she wouldn't want to be her best friend anymore.

Pearl grabbed her bag from the empty classroom, and tiptoed along the dusky corridor into the cloakroom. Thank goodness, no one was there! Then a voice spoke softly from a dark corner.

'Are you all right, Pearl?'

It was Grace.

Pearl lowered her eyes and nodded.

'Come on, then, Mum's waiting outside for us.'

Grace still wanted to be friends!

Pearl looked up gratefully. 'Oh Grace – thank you – but I don't think I can come to tea today…will you tell your mum I'm sorry?'

And before she disgraced herself with more tears, Pearl grabbed her jacket and ran – down the corridors and through the main front door.

There on the steps, blocking her way, stood Amy Perkins.

'Thief,' she hissed. 'I always knew you was no good, Pearl Lovett. You better watch out, girls who steal get put away.'

Pearl pushed past her and ran blindly home.

She stood at the garden gate for a while, and took a deep breath.

The front door shot open, and Jenny appeared. 'Oh, hello Pearl! I thought you were going to tea with Grace? Anyway, come on in chicken, I've got something to tell you.' She took Pearl's bag from her. 'Come and sit on the sofa a minute, love, and have a drink.'

She knelt down by Pearl, and took her hands gently into her own. 'Pearl, we've just had a phone call from social services…you're not to worry, dear, but it seems your mum has gone missing from the hospital…'

Chapter 5

That night sleep would not come. Frozen with fear, Pearl lay in bed, her head swimming.

She was in terrible trouble. In the morning there would be a letter on the doormat telling Jenny that Pearl was a thief.

And then Bernie would come, and be so sad, and say they were very disappointed in her. And she would take her away to a Home...

Pearl shuddered, her hands cold and clammy with sweat.

And her mum had gone missing.

What should she do?

Pearl turned restlessly from side to side.

One thing was sure – she didn't want to be there when that letter arrived.

Perhaps she could get up early and hide the letter before Jenny found it? Then she remembered that the post came after she went to school.

And why had Mum run away?

Perhaps they were treating her badly at the hospital.

And then, suddenly, Pearl had it.

It was the letter she had written to Mum! Mum had run away so she could come and rescue her – before she was adopted and lost forever.

And there was only one place she would run to – the boat!

Pearl sat bolt upright in bed.

It was so obvious; why hadn't she thought of it before? Mum was – this very minute – making her way back to the boat. Then she would come secretly and fetch Pearl, and before anyone could stop them they would be off and away down the canals!

Mum knew the canals like the back of her hand. They could disappear together and never be found!

It was clear to Pearl what she should do.

She should run away to join Mum on the boat!

Her heart leaped with excitement. Her head whirled with ideas.

In the morning, she would pretend to go off to school as usual, but instead she would make her way back home to Leicestershire.

How would she get there?

In a flash it came to her. She could go by train! She had been saving all her pocket money since she came to live with Jenny, to buy a special birthday present for Mum. Quietly she got out of bed, and opened the drawer where she kept her money box.

She clicked on the bedside light, and counted out her money; good, fifteen pounds.

Surely that was enough to get her back home?

That night Pearl laid her plans.

When Jenny called her in the morning, Pearl got dressed quickly. She put on her warmest clothes; it was very mild, but it was December, so she was taking no chances.

Then very carefully, she took out all the books from the box in the wardrobe.

The one book that was hers – her beautiful poetry book, that Mum had given her for Christmas last year – she packed lovingly in her school bag.

Hot with shame, she placed the others on her duvet, in a neat row. She tried to rub out what she had written on the front page, but it was Biro and it wouldn't come out. So she blacked out the awful words as carefully as she could. She could not bear anyone to see them. Jenny would be sure to find the books later on, and take them back to school.

She felt a flood of relief.

Amy's words: 'Thief! I always knew you was no good, Pearl Lovett!' echoed in her head.

Now they would know she was sorry.

And they couldn't put her away in a Home.

Pearl sat at the breakfast table, pushing her toast round and round her plate.

'You haven't eaten a thing, Pearl!' Jenny's worried voice broke into her feverish thoughts. 'And it's a chilly morning, chick – come on – just one piece of toast and honey.'

Pearl forced down the food.

She put on her padded jacket, her hat and scarf, and picked up her bag.

'Are you all right, love?' Jenny stooped to give her a kiss.

'I'm fine, Jenny, honest,' said Pearl.

But as she ran down the front garden path, guilt swept over her.

She was glad – oh so glad – to be heading for home, but Jenny had been very good to her…

No! She mustn't think like that. In a moment that letter would arrive, and then Jenny wouldn't like her any more.

Pearl ran along the street to the cross roads.

But instead of turning left towards school as she usually did, she turned right towards the bus stop that would take her into town, and the station. She knew where the station was, because Jenny had taken her to London one day for a special treat.

But this time, she would be going home!

Pearl heard a bus in the distance, and sprinted the last few yards to the stop.

'Town, please!' she said, holding out a fifty pence coin.

'Where's your mum?' said the driver. 'Are you on your own today?'

'Oh – yes – Mum said I can go to school on my own, now,' Pearl fibbed.

Now she was telling porky-pies, too!

She found a seat at the back, where no one would ask her questions.

And as they bumped and jolted all the way to the city centre, a drum began to beat in Pearl's brain.

'Home, going home!' beat the drum. 'Home, home, home!'

And suddenly she wasn't afraid any more.

It was a short walk from the bus station to the train station. Pearl remembered the way they had gone to catch the London train. By now the sun was up and Pearl was beginning to feel very warm. She turned into the station.

Noise, everywhere. Loudspeakers booming, saying words no one could understand.

Crowds of people, all knowing where they were going.

'Lost your Mum, have you?' An old lady, all smiles and white bobbing curls was peering down at her.

'Oh – no – Mum's over there, thank you!'

Pearl ran towards the crowd, and disappeared into it as fast as she could.

She was getting very good at porky-pies.

The crowd was staring up at a huge overhead notice board, with brightly lit words.

It said DEPARTURES.

Pearl stared at the board. No mention of Leicester.

A wave of panic started in her stomach and rippled through her whole body. For a moment her eyes wouldn't focus. Then she made herself scan the whole board slowly. And suddenly, there it was, hiding under a list of other place names:

`LEEDS 10:05`   `PLATFORM 4`
`CALLING AT`
`LUTON`
`KETTERING`
`MARKET HARBOROUGH`
`LEICESTER`

She was in good time!

Pearl fished inside her bag for her purse.

Surely fifteen pounds would be enough?

She would go up to the counter, just as Jenny had the day they went to London, and say, 'A *day return to Leicester, please.*'

Then she thought about the bus driver.

'*On your own today, are you?*'

And the kind old lady: '*Lost your mum have you?*'

No – people would be sure to ask questions.

For a moment her heart sank.

Then a brilliant idea came to her.

There were parents and children all over the place.

What if she tagged on behind someone, and pretended she belonged to them.

'Yes,' said Pearl out loud. 'Yes, that's what I'll do.'

Quietly she mingled in the crowd, and followed the drift towards platform four.

Ahead of her she saw a mother with a toddler in a pushchair.

If I tag onto her, she won't notice, thought Pearl. *She'll be so busy with all those bags and the pushchair, she won't see me.*

Pearl trailed down the steps after the pushchair lady.

She kept close, but not too close, just behind her.

When they reached the platform the little boy started to howl and the lady bent to comfort him.

Pearl slid behind a station wagon piled high with boxes, and waited. The lady took the little boy out of the pushchair, and started to fold it up.

Pearl glanced at the station clock.

10:04: any minute now!

Suddenly there was a boom and a crackle, and a voice

announced:

'The train arriving at Platform Four is the 10:05 for Leeds, calling at Luton, Kettering, Market Harborough, Leicester…'

In the distance she heard faint tapping on the tracks growing stronger and stronger, and then with a roar and a blast of hot oily air, the train screeched into the station.

The mother shoved the pushchair under one arm, and held the toddler close.

For a second Pearl nearly went to help her, because the little boy was struggling, and the mother was having problems with her luggage, too. But then she remembered she must be invisible.

She followed the lady to the train door.

'Can I help you with that pushchair?'

It was a tall young lady with a knapsack on her back.

'Oh, thank you so much!' sighed the pushchair lady, and as they were helped onto the train, Pearl slipped, silent as a ghost, behind her, and turned quickly into the next carriage.

Down the train she walked – quickly, but not running.

Where should she go?

Where would no one notice her?

Then she had it! *Find it quickly*, said the voice in her head, *before anyone sees you.*

And there it was. The door marked TOILET.

She darted inside, shot the bolt, and leaned up against

the door shakily.

It had worked!

With a sigh of relief, she sat down on the loo and put her bag on the floor. Then the toilet seat shook violently, and they were off!

Home, going home, home, home, home, sang the drum in Pearl's ears, and the train track answered: *home in a bit, home in a bit, home in a bit, home!*

Chapter 6

'WE ARE NOW APPROACHING LEICESTER STATION,' said the announcer's voice. 'PASSENGERS FOR BIRMINGHAM PLEASE...'

At last.

Pearl stood up and rubbed her bottom. The loo seat had bumped and banged her all the way to Leicester. And a lot of people had been very annoyed with her, too.

'How much longer are you going to be in there?' said a very bad-tempered lady. 'I've been waiting ten minutes already!'

Others had just shaken the door and gone crossly on their way.

And once Pearl heard a voice shout, 'Tickets please!' She had crouched, silent and and trembling, but the footsteps tramped right past her and away down the next carriage.

That had been the worst moment of all. Pearl shivered

when she thought what would have happened to her if she had been caught without a ticket.

The train turned into a bend and braked hard then slowed almost to a stop.

Pearl got to her feet and grabbed her bag.

She took a deep breath and stepped out into the corridor. All around her were legs and feet. She squeezed herself gently behind a very tall man, her heart pounding.

He didn't even notice.

The doors banged open, and Pearl found herself carried along with everyone else. She climbed down onto the platform, and moved with the crowd.

'Are you all right?' It was the lady with the curly white hair again. 'Where's your mum now?'

'Oh…she's just ahead!'

Pearl squeezed herself through the crowd and ran. Up the steps she bounded, and over the bridge.

What would happen if someone asked to see her ticket now?

She saw a family with two little girls ahead, and tagged on behind them. But there was no ticket collector – just the open foyer, and then the pale lemon sunshine of a December day.

She'd done it!

A wave of relief flowed over her; here she was, back in Leicester! The centre was bright with Christmas decorations. Pearl felt a pang of anguish; this would be her first Christmas ever away from Mum. She knew Jenny had been busy hiding away mysterious little parcels, but it wouldn't be the same.

Pearl knew this part of the city very well. Nanna had lived just round the corner from the station. And from there it was only a short walk to the bus that took her out into the countryside, to the canal, and home.

Pearl knew just where the boat would be at this time of the year. In the winter they had always stayed close to the locks at Boxton, so they could be near Nanna for Christmas. They had their own special mooring place, tucked away in a quiet corner.

Then when spring came, off they would go, along the canals to her very favourite place – where the little elderberry tree waited for them, all dressed in palest gold, magic, wonderful…

Pearl trotted along the streets to the bus station.

Just round the corner was Nanna's house, only Nanna wasn't there any more…

They never went back to the house after Nanna died. Neither of them could bear to see it, an empty shell without the warm, smiling presence that had made it alive.

Pearl jerked herself out of her thoughts.

She mustn't think about Nanna. Not now.

The 86 bus was already in the bus station. Pearl checked the time on the station clock.

1:20.

She knew the 86 bus left at half past the hour, so she went into the little cafe to get warm.

'All on your own, are you?'

This time it was an old man.

'Oh no – my mum's just outside!' Pearl fled.

Too many questions!

She hid behind a news' kiosk until there was only a minute to go, and then walked quickly to the bus.

'A child fare to Boxton Locks, please.' She tried to sound firm and confident, as if she did this sort of thing all the time.

The driver paused a moment and raised his eyebrows before he issued the ticket.

'My mum's meeting me at the other end,' said Pearl hastily. 'She says I'm old enough to go on the bus on my own.'

'Does she now? Hmmmm. Well, you be careful, young lady.' The bus driver was giving her a very funny look.

'Oh, I will,' gasped Pearl.

She ran to the end of the bus, and found a single seat over the wheel, where no one could ask her any more awkward questions.

The bus seemed to take forever. It was old and ramshackle, and once it was clear of the town, it wound its way along the lanes, stopping every few minutes. Pearl fretted impatiently, her excitement mounting as she recognised some of the villages.

Soon she would be home!

She saw it all in her mind's eye.

She would run along the lane, over the canal bridge and down the steep path at the side. From there it was only a little way along the towpath till she reached the Marina.

Then she would leap over the little plank onto the deck, and knock on the door, and there would be Mum!

And they would hug and hug, and everything would be all right again...

How surprised Mum would be to see her!

Pearl drifted on the wings of her dream. Suddenly it seemed very warm on the bus, and her eyes *would* keep closing. She felt herself floating far far away...

'Hey, sleepyhead — didn't you say you wanted Boxton Locks? The bus driver's face swam into focus. 'Because if you did, you've missed your stop!'

Pearl jerked out of sleep and sprang to her feet. There was no one else left on the bus.

'Where are we?' she mumbled.

'Bradby!' said the driver. 'But it's only a little way back down the lane to Boxton. You'll do it in about fifteen minutes.'

'Thank you!'

Pearl stumbled down the gangway and off the bus.

'That way!' shouted the driver. 'Are you sure you'll be all right?'

'I'm fine, thank you!'

Pearl set off back to Boxton.

For a moment she didn't know where she was, then she recognised the little village ahead. She and Mum had often come there to the village shop, or sometimes to buy fish and chips.

Fish and chips!

Her mouth watered. She realised suddenly how hungry she was. It had been a long time since breakfast. She checked her watch.

A quarter to three.

She turned into the main street of the village.

The fish and chip shop was closed. But the village shop was open.

The bell clanged as she stepped through the door.

'Hello Pearl! We haven't seen you for a long time!' The shopkeeper smiled down at Pearl. 'You been down to Brinklow again?'

Pearl nodded. She went over to the fridge.

She chose a chicken roll, and a can of coke. Then she bought a packet of Maltesers from the sweet counter. Mum loved Maltesers. She would give them to her as surprise.

'How's your Mum keeping?'

'Oh – fine thank you, fine.' Pearl counted out her money carefully.

'Well, give her my best wishes – and tell her I'd like to

buy some more of those trays she paints – they sell really well!'

'I will.'

Pearl clanged out of the shop, and sat down on a nearby wall.

She munched solidly through her roll and put the Maltesers in her pocket. She finished off with a long drink of coke.

That was better.

Then she set off down the road back to Boxton.

It was when she came to the stile by Newlands Farm that Pearl remembered the short cut. There was a path through the woods that cut out a big loop in the road. It would save a lot of time.

Pearl stopped and thought.

It was getting on for four o'clock. It was winter.

Soon it would be dark.

Overhead a flock of starlings made for the city to roost. She watched for a moment, as they swirled and melted into ever-changing patterns – like a shoal of dark shining fish. The air was full of their shrill silvery calls.

A chill wind whirled through the trees. Pearl shivered.

Perhaps she should stick to the road.

Then she had a thought. Soon Jenny would wonder why she hadn't come home from school. There would be phone calls.

No – best get back to Mum as soon as possible, then they could make off down the canals together in the dark, and no one would ever find them.

Quickly she climbed over the stile, and into the darkening wood.

Chapter 7

The wood was full of voices.

At first they were happy voices – the honeyed carollings of a robin, little scribbles from a wren, and then the rich fluting voice of a blackbird.

They cheered her on her way. It wasn't until she was deep in the shadows of tall trees that she felt the first flickerings of unease. Slowly the light thickened, and one by one the birds stopped singing.

A dog barked, making her jump; then she remembered that the wood skirted the edge of Newlands Farm. It would only be Old Flossie, the collie. She thought of the times she and Mum had walked into the farmyard to buy eggs. Old Flossie would be barking her head off, but her tail always wagged furiously at the same time.

'Don't you mind her, me duck – she's soft as a cowpat!' Mrs Smith used to say.

She smiled at the memory.

But then new sounds came from the wood – scurryings and rustlings.

In the undergrowth twigs snapped.

Rats!

She remembered Mum saying, 'You're never more than four yards away from a rat!' and laughing when she saw the look on Pearl's face.

She'd never really worried about things like that when Mum was around. The countryside teemed with life – little water voles in the canal banks, badgers, foxes prowling round the boats looking for scraps, rabbits, birds, dragonflies... Pearl loved them all.

It had all seemed so safe.

But on your own, with night falling, somehow it felt very different.

And then Pearl admitted it to herself.

It really was dark.

And she was scared.

'Not far to go now!' she said out loud. Hearing her own voice made her feel stronger.

Any minute now she would come to the little bridge over the stream, where she and Mum used to play Pooh sticks, when she was little...

She stopped. Surely she should have reached the bridge long ago?

She peered through the twilight.

She recognised nothing. A wave of panic flowed over her.

Quickly she turned to retrace her footsteps.

She broke into a little jog trot, her breath coming in frightened gasps. A branch from a tree whipped back and caught her in the face.

She stopped to rub her cheek, panting.

Steady!

It was stupid to run in the dark. She could easily twist her foot in a rabbit hole and sprain her ankle. She forced herself to walk carefully, trying to push back the rising tide of terror that threatened to drown her.

Pearl felt her legs give way beneath her. She sank to the ground, not noticing the cold and the scratchy brambles.

She took a few deep, shuddering breaths.

'All right, I'm lost!' she said to the darkness.

There! She had said it.

But if she didn't give in, if she kept on looking, sooner or later she would find the little bridge, and then she would know where she was. She rubbed her legs, willing some strength back into them. If only there was a moon.

For a while she crashed around uselessly in the undergrowth, looking for the main path. It was very tiring pushing your way through thickets and brambles. But she plodded on determinedly. Somewhere very near here was the canal, and her home – and Mum, a well Mum, all smiling and rosy cheeked like she used to be.

That thought kept Pearl going.

When the branches from the hazel trees smacked her

in the face, and the brambles tore at her legs, she kept in front of her, always, the picture of her mother's face, and she heard her say: 'Oh Pearl, I knew you would make it!'

It wasn't until she went flying over an old tree stump, and landed flat on her face in a pool of icy water that Pearl admitted to herself that she wasn't going to make it that night.

She tried to get to her feet, but fell back with a cry.

A pain like fire shot through her ankle. She rubbed her eyes furiously.

She would not cry!

A wave of panic swept over her. She screwed her eyes tight shut, and thought of her mother, waiting for her there on the boat, only a short distance away. Pearl took a deep, shuddering breath, and dragged herself out of the mud onto higher ground.

She would have to spend the night in the wood, until first light. Then surely she would recognise where she was, and maybe, if she rested her ankle, she would be able to walk again.

Suddenly she felt calm.

OK. She was in a wood on her own.

It was dark, and she was afraid.

But people in story books were always facing terrible dangers. One of her favourite stories came into her head. It was about about a boy who ran away to an island. He had made a shelter out of slender branches of willow.

Pearl remembered exactly how he had done it.

First he had cut the branches and stuck them in the ground in a circle. Then he tied them all together at the top with string. Finally he wove thin branches in and out of the frame to fill in the gaps. And there was a little hut! It was magic because leaves grew on the branches, and made a living green home.

Pearl had loved that story. Often at night she would lie in bed and imagine herself onto that island. Of course Jack – that was his name, Jack – had done all this in daylight, and he hadn't hurt his ankle, but just thinking about it made her feel warmer.

For she had to admit it; she was very cold.

She couldn't do what Jack had done, but she could make herself some sort of shelter.

She took off her scarf and tied it tightly round her ankle.

Good; that felt much better.

She stood up carefully, and found she could hobble a little by clinging onto the hazel branches. Perhaps if she crept deep inside the undergrowth it would be warmer there?

She crawled on her hands and knees for a while. The ground seemed to be going upwards a bit. Suddenly she bumped her head.

She had gone smack into a tree trunk. She pushed herself up, holding onto the rough, wet bark.

Her fingers slipped into space.

She felt around the tree trunk as far as she could. It was wide, so wide that both of her outstretched arms reached only a small section of it. The space was a big hole in the trunk.

It was a huge, hollow tree!

Carefully she edged backwards into the tree's softly ribbed inside. There was a moment's panic when she wondered what – or who – might be inside.

Nothing – just a large, empty space. She slipped her hands over the silky bark.

Then she breathed in the fragrance of fern and leaf, and old wood. The inside of the tree was thick with dry, scrunchy leaves. And it was warm. She curled up into a tight little ball.

It felt as if the tree was holding her in strong, safe arms.

Pearl fell into an exhausted sleep.

Chapter 8

It was the robin who woke her.

Pearl lay in the velvet dark of the hollow tree. The sweet, liquid piping pierced the shadows, trill upon trill, golden loops of sound.

For a moment she thought she was back on the boat. She stretched, and her hand hit solid wood. Pearl realised she was very cold and damp. Shivering, she rubbed her aching limbs.

A pain shot through her ankle, and snapshots of the previous day flashed into her mind. She sat up and massaged her ankle gently. Then she peered through the doorway of her little shelter.

All around her was a soft grey light.

It was day.

Pearl rebound her ankle firmly with the scarf. Then very carefully, she edged out into the wood.

A spider's web hung like a pearly curtain in front of her

doorway. She brushed it gently aside. Dewdrops shivered silver in the half light.

The wood was full of bird song.

She stood up gingerly, steadying herself against a hazel bush. This time the pain wasn't so bad. She remembered that the ground before her hollow oak had risen slowly. Perhaps if she climbed a little higher, she might see where she was?

As she crawled through the bushes, she saw that the mist was slowly lifting. Low in the sky, a pale sun swam through the clouds. Then the clouds parted and brilliant light poured over her.

It seemed like a gift – something wonderful...

She stretched out her hands to feel the faint warmth.

Now she could see where she was going!

Pearl limped determinedly to the top of the little hill. There, below her, was a clearing, and flowing through the middle, a ferny stream.

If she followed it, she would eventually reach the little bridge where she and her mum used to play Pooh sticks!

Pearl slid down the little hollow on her bottom. It wasn't until she reached the stream that she realised how thirsty she was.

Thirsty, and cold – so very cold.

Should she drink from the stream? Mum had always told her that you couldn't trust stream water nowadays – too many nasty chemicals seeping into the water from the fields.

Pearl's thirst grew desperate. Her tongue was sticking horribly to the roof of her mouth. Chemicals or no chemicals, she would have to drink. She bent over the stream and scooped the bubbling water into her hands. It was icy cold, but so sweet!

She gulped mouthful after mouthful.

Ah, that was so good! If only she had saved some of yesterday's food. Then she remembered the packet of Maltesers for her mum.

Mum wouldn't mind if she ate a few.

It was difficult to open the packet – her fingers were stiff and clumsy with cold. She tipped four Maltesers into her hand, and ate them slowly, one at a time.

Pearl thought they were the best things she had ever eaten.

With a rush of energy, she got to her feet, and started to trace the path of the stream.

Then she stopped. Supposing she was going the wrong way along the stream? How did she know which way the bridge would be? For a moment she hesitated, then turned downstream. She would walk for a little while, and see if she recognized anything.

Her foot began to throb again. If only she had a stick to lean on. She tried to break a branch from a little ash tree, but the wood was young and springy, and wouldn't snap.

And then she saw it – a fallen branch, just the right size.

Pearl got along much better with her stick. There was a

sort of fork at the top, and she found that if she shoved it under her arm, like a crutch, she could take the weight off her ankle. She was still cold, but the exercise warmed her, and she stopped shivering.

Suddenly she heard the sound of bubbling water.

A waterfall!

Pearl's heart leapt for joy. There was a little waterfall near the bridge; some boys had dammed the stream one summer, and she had added stones to it herself.

She pressed onwards fiercely, ignoring the pain in her ankle.

Yes – there it was; a little pool glinted in the silvery light, and there, a few metres downstream, was her bridge.

Pearl stood panting on the old wooden planks. To her left was the path that led down towards the canal. She set off joyfully, her heart singing. In a few moments she would see the canal, and then home, and Mum!

The woodland path twisted sharply to the left – and there was the gap in the hedge that came out onto the tow path. Carefully, she pushed through the prickly hawthorn.

There, pale gold in the sunrise, lay the canal, and the path that led to the Marina.

It was still very early in the morning. There was no sign of life anywhere on the canal bank. She hobbled painfully down the steep path that led past the locks. Ahead of her a dozen or so boats bobbed gently in the big round pool of the marina. Greedily she drank in the friendly smell of oil and paint and reedy water. Smoke came from one chimney, but most of the curtains were still drawn.

Good; no one would see her.

It was then that the full realisation of what she had done dawned on Pearl; for a moment she felt a pang of guilt about Jenny, but she pushed it to the back of her mind. One thing was sure, though – a lot of people would be looking for her. What if the police had guessed where she was going!

She hurried on along the tow path, past the silent boats and the little gift shop where Mum sold her canal ware. The *ELDERFLOWER* was always moored away from the main part of the marina, in a quiet spot.

Pearl squinted her eyes against the low December sun.

There ahead of her was a boat. On the roof were three little window boxes. In the sunshine the paint gleamed brightly – blue, gold and white. Her own boat, her own home, the *ELDERFLOWER*!

On the bow, a little blossom tree nodded gently in the breeze.

Pearl felt a surge of new strength flow through her body. She hobbled the last few metres at breakneck speed. Then she threw down her crutch, climbed painfully over the side of the boat, and slid down the wooden step to the tiny doors.

They were locked.

Of course – they would be at this time of day.

Pearl rattled the lock impatiently. Pain shot up her leg, but in her excitement it didn't seem to matter.

'Mum! Mum! It's me! It's Pearl!'

The boat rocked as someone came to the door. She heard the sound of bolts being drawn back.

The door opened.

A tall, black lady gazed down upon her with astonishment.

'What the…? Oh heck!' she said.

The world darkened, and dizzy and exhausted, Pearl fell down the steps into the saloon.

Chapter 9

Pearl was drowning in a dark sea. She tried to open her eyes, but they wouldn't obey her. Somewhere a long way off a voice echoed in the darkness. She struggled once more to open her eyes.

Slowly the darkness faded, and through the mist a face swam into focus

A dark, golden face, that smiled warmly at her.

'My goodness, you gave me a fright!' said the voice.

Pearl felt a wave of nausea flow over her.

Then it passed, and slowly the face came into focus.

It was a pretty face – round, smiling, darker than she was, with long, rippling hair.

But not Mum – oh, not her mum.

'I thought – I thought you'd be my mum,' whispered Pearl. 'But you're not!'

She felt a rush of tears to her eyes.

'I'm very sorry,' said the lady. 'No, I'm not your mum;

but I think I know who you are. You must be Pearl.'

Pearl struggled to sit up, but the nausea came flooding back. She sank back onto a cool pillow.

Then she realised where she was.

She was lying on a bed – *her own bed*, in her own cabin. And at the window were the bluebird curtains.

Panic seized her.

'How do you know my name?' she gasped. 'And where's my mum!'

'I know your name, Pearl, because yesterday afternoon this boat was crawling with police and social workers looking for you! But I'm afraid I don't know where your mum is.'

Pearl sat bolt upright. 'The police knew to come here?'

'I'm afraid so, Pearl. It was the first place they thought of looking. Of course, I told them I hadn't seen you – but they checked the village shop, and they've been asking everyone questions.'

Pearl struggled to her feet.

'I must go!' she gasped. 'Before they find me!'

A strong and gentle hand pushed her back firmly onto the bed.

'I don't think you're fit to go anywhere at the moment, Pearl. Look, why don't you come on into the saloon, and I'll make you a nice warm drink. And then I'd better have a look at that ankle.'

'Are you going to ring the police?' asked Pearl.

'No – I'm going to make you a hot drink, and some breakfast. You look terrible!'

Pearl allowed herself to be helped into the saloon, and tucked up in the rocking chair, with her foot raised on a little stool.

Her rocking chair!

Her eyes wandered round the saloon.

There was the little wood stove, burning brightly.

There was her mother's cane chair, with the peacock cushions. At the windows were the curtains she had helped Mum tie-dye, green and blue as the sea.

On one window hung the peacock Mum had painted one long, cold winter. On the other side of the cabin, light streamed through a stained glass rainbow and splashed the floor crimson, purple and blue.

The same! Everything was the same!

But where was Mum? And what was this strange young lady doing in their boat?

'Right you are, Pearl.' A tray appeared in front of her.

There was a mug of chocolate, and a plate of hot buttered toast and honey. A rush of saliva told Pearl how hungry, how very hungry she was.

She sipped the chocolate, and felt its warmth seeping through her. Then she fell upon the toast.

But suddenly, she had had enough. Her stomach tightened, and she pushed the tray away from her. A terrible tiredness came over her, and she felt her nose prickle with the tears that would keep coming.

The lady sat down beside her. For a moment her hand reached out as if to stroke Pearl's hair, but then she pulled back.

'You must have had quite a night of it, Pearl. Do you want to tell me about it?'

Pearl looked up into the deep brown eyes. Kindness and concern shone down upon her.

'Who are you?' whispered Pearl.

'My name's Amber.'

Pearl looked at the honey-gold skin, and the warm eyes.

And in a rush she knew that she could trust this kind stranger, and that she wanted to tell her everything.

Pearl took a deep breath, and poured out her story to Amber.

She told her how she had lived so happily on the boat with Mum. And how much Mum had loved her, and always taken such good care of her.

But then Mum had got ill, and the doctor said she had to go to hospital, because she was so poorly.

'They had no need to take her away,' said Pearl, her voice wobbling. 'I looked after her when she was sick, we were fine without them interfering!'

She told Amber about Jenny and Bernie, and how they wanted to find her a Forever Family. And how she had written to her mum, telling her to get better quickly, before someone adopted her, and took her away for ever.

And then she told Amber about the stolen books, and how she had been found out. And how Jenny had told her that very same day that Mum had gone missing from the hospital.

And all the time Amber listened, and looked at her with those kind, dark eyes.

'So you see, I *had* to run away, or they would have put me in a Home,' whispered Pearl. 'And I was so sure Mum would be here, waiting for me, 'specially after she got my letter. Else why would she run away?'

Then suddenly everything came to a head, and all the tears Pearl had held back when she was alone in the woods, afraid and in pain, came pouring out, and she cried and cried, until she had no tears left.

Amber took Pearl's hand gently into her own.

'Pearl, you are one of the bravest girls I have ever met. But I don't know why your mum ran away – and yes, maybe she is looking for you. But she certainly hasn't been here. And you know, Pearl, a lot of people are very fond of you, and are very worried about you at the moment. Don't you think maybe I should give them a ring and tell them you're safe?'

She picked up her mobile and switched it on.

'NO!'

Pearl leaped to her feet, gasping with pain.

'They'll put me in a Home, Amber! I know they will. I've got to find my mum, and then everything will be all right.'

She glared at Amber. 'If you phone anyone, I'll run away again. I will, you know!'

Amber put the phone down with a sigh.

'Whatever am I going to do with you, Pearl? It's really important to tell everyone you're safe, you know. Your foster mother must be so worried.'

For a moment Pearl wavered: she really did not want to upset Jenny. Then she thought about her real mother, out there somewhere, waiting for her.

'I want to find my mum. Help me find her, *please* Amber!'

Then a sudden idea struck her.

'I know – I know where Mum will be! We always used to spend Christmas here at Boxton, so we could be near Nanna, but…but after Nanna died, sometimes we went down to Broughton for the winter! That's where my special magic tree is – you know, the one the boat's named after. Me and Mum really loved that tree – maybe she's gone there!'

'Pearl, do you realise that I could get into terrible trouble if I don't phone the police and say I've found you? There's a law against that sort of thing!'

Pearl felt her lips tremble. 'I just can't go back, Amber – I can't. It's all right for you – I bet no one ever tried to put you in a Home!'

'Ah, that's where you're wrong, Pearl. I spent most of my childhood in Children's Homes – one crappy

Home after another.'

'You grew up in Children's Homes?' Pearl was shocked to the core. 'Didn't you have a mum?'

'Oh yes, I had a mum all right, Pearl. But she wasn't like yours. She preferred her lousy boyfriend to me. Said I was too much trouble, and I was ruining the only chance she'd ever have of love.'

'So she put you in a Home?' Pearl whispered.

'Yep. I was eight at the time, and after that I bounced from one stinking Home to another. They tried foster parents, but everyone said I was, "Too difficult – too damaged – too disturbed."'

Pearl sat in horrified silence.

Eventually, she found her voice. 'Did you ever run away?'

'Yep – lots of times – and they always caught me, and then I ended up in a worse Home than ever.'

'That's what they'll do to me, won't they, now I've done something bad?'

'I suppose they might,' said Amber. 'But I don't think what you did was all that bad, Pearl; after all, you only did it because you missed your mum so much, didn't you? They might still try and find you a good foster home, you know.'

'*I don't want no foster home*,' said Pearl between gritted teeth. 'I don't want no Forever Family neither. *I want my own mum back*. And if you won't help me, I'll find her myself!'

Pearl made towards the cabin door, but her legs suddenly gave way, and she had to clutch hold of the side of the boat. Amber put her arm round her shoulder, and led her gently back to the rocking chair.

'You really are one determined girl, aren't you,' she sighed.

Then she took a deep breath.

'OK, Pearl. YOU don't run away, and I'll take you down to Broughton on the boat, and we'll see if your mother's there. And if she is, that's fine – and if she's not, I phone the police. Agreed?'

'Oh thank you, thank you, Amber!' For a moment Pearl wanted to give Amber a hug, but she felt too shy. 'I know Mum'll be there, I know she will!'

'Hmm.' Amber rubbed her nose thoughtfully.

Then she smiled. 'If we're going to Broughton, Pearl, the sooner we're off the better. Any minute now the police could be back. Although I guess they've probably switched their search away from the canals to the area around that hospital where your mum was. They probably think you'll be looking for her there.'

'That's miles from here,' smiled Pearl 'Over Birmingham way.'

'Still, we won't take any chances. And the first thing you can do is have a shower. You have absolutely no idea what you look like!'

*

It was lovely being back in her own tiny bathroom. The boat was a modernised one, with a little galley for cooking, and a separate shower and loo. Amber put an old stool in the shower because Pearl's ankle hurt too much to stand up, gave her some gorgeous smelling shower lotion and left her to it. She rightly guessed that Pearl would want to be on her own.

Fifteen minutes later Pearl emerged shiningly clean and smelling sweetly of spicy flowers. Amber had brushed most of the mud off her clothes, although Pearl had to make do with yesterday's underwear.

'I'm afraid mine won't fit you!' laughed Amber. 'And now it's time to have a look at that ankle.'

Amber felt Pearl's ankle with gentle fingers. 'Can you wriggle your toes?'

Pearl wriggled.

'Can you draw a circle with your big toe?'

Pearl tried gingerly. 'Ow – that hurts!'

'Hmm. I'm pretty sure you haven't broken it, Pearl – I think it's just a bad sprain. Which means we need a bag of frozen peas!'

Amber ferreted around in the little box freezer. 'No peas – mixed veg will have to do!'

She tucked the frozen packet round Pearl's ankle.

'Oh!' gasped Pearl. 'That feels so good!'

'Right,' said Amber. 'Let's get going!'

Pearl was eager to help. 'I always used to steer the boat

74

while Mum did the locks,' she said.

'Pearl, you can't do anything with that ankle. And you're going to have to keep below deck – don't you realise that half the police forces of England are looking for you!'

Pearl hadn't thought about that. 'I can cook, though, when my ankle's better. And I'm really good at washing up.'

'Brilliant.' Amber busied herself with a few last minute jobs.

And then Pearl heard a sound that nearly stopped her heart.

A loud and insistent mew!

'About time too,' said Amber, opening the saloon doors.

And in walked Tiggy.

For a moment both cat and child froze.

And then Tiggy was in her arms, butting her hard, furry little head against Pearl's, gazing at her with those deep emerald eyes, and purring and purring.

Tears of joy poured down Pearl's face and onto Tiggy's gold spangled fur.

'I think you two must know each other,' said Amber, and she rubbed her nose briskly.

Chapter 10

Pearl sat in the rocking chair, Tiggy snoozing blissfully on her lap, and her foot comfortably supported. The frozen veg had done a great job. The pain and swelling were beginning to subside, and as she felt better, Pearl began to think.

A hundred questions formed in her mind.

What was Amber doing on their boat?

Had Mum sold it?

Then why were so many things the same?

And the biggest question of all: where was Mum?

Was she searching for her, worried out of her mind, this very minute? Or was she down at Broughton, waiting impatiently for Pearl to arrive?

Perhaps – and here was an alarming thought – she had gone to Jenny's house to pick her up?

But of course, she couldn't do that, could she? The social workers would never let her. No, the more she thought about it, the more certain Pearl was that her mum had gone down to Broughton, to wait by their favourite spot underneath the magic elderberry tree.

There was no way of getting an answer to the first three questions, because Amber was at the stern of the boat, busy steering them through the canal network to Broughton.

And she had forbidden Pearl to even poke her nose through the door. Questions would have to wait until Amber paused for lunch.

For a time, Pearl occupied herself peeping out of the window. It was so lovely to be afloat again. She realised how much she had missed the waterworld which had always been there, lapping her softly and safely from her earliest days.

She gazed out of the window, relishing everything – the smell of water and reeds, the sparrows squabbling in the scarlet-berried hedgerows, parties of ducks gliding alongside the boat, two white horses startled by a passing train, galloping wildly, silver manes flaring in the sunlight.

Her world – her precious world.

And all the time she stroked Tiggy, letting her hands glide over the silky fur, giving her the special head to tail stroke she liked so much, and then finishing off by a gentle tickle under her chin.

'I never forgot you, Tiggy,' she whispered. 'I swore I'd come back and find you one day.'

She fished in her bag, and pulled out her only remaining book – the poetry book that really and truly was her very own. She read aloud, savouring the words, while Tiggy stretched and purred. Lulled by the lapping water, warm and comfortable, all her pain and weariness drained away. The book fell from her fingers, and Pearl slept.

'Hi, sleepyhead! Are you too tired for lunch?' Amber's smiling face swam into view.

'Oh, Amber – *I* was going to get lunch for us!'

'Too late! Do you like Scotch pancakes?'

'Scotch pancakes are my *fave* things!' Pearl gazed with pleasure at the plate set before her; Scotch pancakes with lemon and raisins, salmon sandwiches and an apple.

She ate hungrily. Then she noticed something. 'This is my own plate – the one Nanna gave me when I was little!'

Pearl looked at the plate with its smiling giraffe and cuddly tigers. It was a baby's plate – but just seeing it made her feel warm all over.

'Amber – can I ask you some questions?' she asked shyly. 'I don't mean to be rude, but there's so much I don't understand!'

'That's all right – fire away!'

'Well, first of all,' said Pearl slowly, 'how come you're in our boat – and how come everything's *just the same*?'

'It's no mystery, really, Pearl,' said Amber gently. 'When your mum had to go into hospital, she decided to sell the boat and everything in it.'

'What – oh – you met my mum!'

'No. No, Pearl. Your mum put the boat into the hands of an agent. I saw it and fell in love with it. It was perfect – just what I wanted. I never met your mum – everything was done through the agent, you see. And the reason I kept most things the same was I just loved them! Of course all the furnishings – things like the curtains and the furniture stayed on the boat. Your mum would have no need for them, would she?'

'Then you mean – you mean she was never coming back to the boat?' Pearl felt a wave of panic flow over her. 'But I thought – I always thought when Mum was better, like, she'd come and get me, and we'd go back home again!'

Pearl felt herself dangerously close to tears again. She mustn't cry all the time, she really mustn't – Amber would think she was such a crybaby!

'I think your mum must have known that she was much too poorly to look after you, or the boat, for a long time, Pearl. Maybe she put the money in the bank, and hoped that one day, when she was much better, she could buy another boat, and have you back again.'

Pearl hadn't thought of that; her heart began to beat wildly with hope. 'Maybe that's what she's going to do, Amber! Maybe that's why she's run away. Perhaps she's been to the bank, and got out the money, and she's waiting

79

for me down at Broughton with a new boat!'

'Perhaps,' said Amber gently. And she smiled a kind, but sad, smile.

Pearl felt much better. 'And another thing, Amber – how come Tiggy's with you?'

'No mystery there, Pearl, either. Shortly after I bought the boat, I heard this mewing at the door. I opened it, and in walks Tiggy, bold as brass. "Well, who are you?" I said. Then she rubbed herself round and round my legs, and jumped onto the rocking chair as if she'd been there all her life! "Ah ha!" I said, "I guess you're the ship's cat!" Anyway, I asked all round the marina about her, and everyone said she had belonged to the lady on the ELDERFLOWER, and her little girl. No one seemed to want her, and she was so sweet, and so determined to stay, I decided to adopt her!'

'I'm so glad you did!' Pearl lifted Tiggy into her arms and gave her a kiss on her head. 'Bernie – that's my social worker – she said they'd found Tiggy a nice home, and I was mad, really mad! They had no right to do that.'

'Perhaps Tiggy ran away, like you, and decided to come home all by herself. She was very thin when she first arrived, so perhaps she'd been making her way home for a long time.'

'So we both came home!' laughed Pearl.

'Why did you call her Tiggy?' Amber tickled Tiggy behind the ears.

'Well, you see, when I first saw her, all splotched with gold, and black and white, I thought she looked just like one of those flowers that you see in florist's shops. Mum said they're called tiger lilies. So we called her Tiger Lily at first, but it's an awful mouthful, so she ended up being called just Tiggy!'

Amber laughed. 'You'll never guess what I called her! I called her Splodge, after that little black patch on her nose! But she answers to anything when you open a tin of sardines!'

'Well, she's Tiggy,' said Pearl firmly. 'My Tiggy.'

'I can see that,' said Amber. 'Anyway, time to be on our way again… I reckon it'll take about three days to get down to the marina at Broughton, so long as we don't have any hold-ups. And I want to find a good mooring place for tonight before it gets dark.'

'There's a good straight bit about a mile past Shardlow,' said Pearl. 'It's nice and quiet, and not too far from the village shops. And the mooring's good – the canal's quite deep near the bank, so you can pull in easy without getting stuck in the mud.'

'You really do know your way about the canals, don't you?' smiled Amber. 'Now, what are you going to do with yourself all afternoon?'

Pearl looked longingly out of the window, and sighed.

'Sorry, Pearl, said Amber. 'I just daren't let you be seen.'

'How are you going to manage the locks on your own?

I always used to hold the boat steady while Mum did the lock.'

'I'll manage the way I always do — on my tod,' said Amber. 'I've already been through three while you were asleep this morning.'

Pearl looked at Amber with admiration.

'One day, when I'm grown up, I'll have my own boat, like you, and I'll travel all over the country by myself.'

'I bet you will!' Amber ruffled Pearl's hair. 'Tell you what — how about me doing your hair for you this evening? I've got some gorgeous extensions; I could make you look really glam.'

'Oh, Amber, would you!' cried Pearl. 'My friend Grace, at school, she had her hair done like that.'

'It's a deal. Now, how would you like to have a go at making yourself a necklace?'

Amber reached into a cardboard box and lifted out a jam jar. It was full of glass beads — crimson, gold, azure, purple, green... There was another jar full of feathers, and little silver stars, and a box full of fastenings. There were spools and spools of coloured thread.

'Oh, Amber, wicked!' Pearl let the beads flow through her fingers like a watery rainbow. She gave a shiver of pleasure.

'Right, that's you settled then. Give me a shout if you have any problems!'

Chapter 11

All that afternoon Pearl arranged and threaded the shining beads. She made a blue and purple necklace that flashed emerald, like a peacock's tail, for her mum. Then she made a starry bracelet for herself. Finally she made a necklace all in gold and black and cinnamon for Amber.

And while she worked, she thought. Part of her was burning with excitement, because every minute that passed brought her nearer to Mum. But there were some uncomfortable, niggling thoughts at the back of her mind that would not go away.

She thought of Jenny and Bernie. Would they be worried about her? Would they miss her? Amber had said, 'There are a lot of people who are really fond of you, Pearl...' She'd never really thought of that before.

But most of all she thought of Grace. 'My friend Grace at school' she had said to Amber. The first proper friend she had ever had. Who had stood by her, even though she knew Pearl was a thief…

Pearl made a great effort and pushed these unpleasant thoughts to the back of her mind. One day she would go back and find Grace, and say she was sorry. But here and now on the boat – her very own boat – with Tiggy purring on her lap, it was hard to feel sad.

Pearl gazed dreamily out of the window. It was late afternoon. The sky burned gold and crimson, and before her the canal lay like a river of fire.

Pearl sighed with pleasure.

Then she jumped to her feet. Soon Amber would be finding their night mooring place. She would be tired and hungry.

I know, thought Pearl, *I'll get her a lovely tea as a surprise*. And she realised that her foot wasn't stabbing anymore, just aching a little.

Pearl hobbled round the galley, looking in all the cupboards, and examining the contents of the tiny fridge.

'Bacon and eggs – and tomatoes, too!'

There was no doubt about it, Amber kept a very well-stocked boat. For a moment a shadow passed over her, as she remembered how often there had been nothing in the fridge when Mum was really sick, and she'd had to ferret in her purse, and see what she could buy for a pound at the village shop. Once for a whole week there was nothing to eat but cornflakes and baked beans.

More bad thoughts. She pinched herself hard, so that the pain would drive them away.

She poured some oil into the frying pan, and within minutes the bacon was sizzling nicely. She found the table mats and the knives and forks in the cupboard where they always used to be. She set the table properly and put out a fresh glass of orange juice for both of them. Very carefully she cut some bread, and buttered it.

And all this time, Tiggy was winding herself round her legs, just as she used to do, reminding Pearl that it was her tea-time too.

Pearl measured out Tiggy's dried catfood, changed her water, and slipped her a tiny bit of bacon.

When Amber came down the steps into the saloon, Pearl had the eggs and tomatoes frying too.

'Wow! I am impressed, Pearl – very impressed! I didn't know you were such a brilliant cook.'

'Tea will be ready in five minutes,' said Pearl shyly.

'Just time for me to get washed up, then.'

Pearl peeped through the curtains. It was really dark now. She could just make out the hedge by the tow path. Overhead a new moon curled low in the sky, slender as the rim of a finger nail. And there was Venus, the evening star, burning with a brilliant blue light. Mum had taught her the names of all the constellations as they sat on deck, warmly wrapped in blankets on crisp, starlit nights.

'Penny for them, Pearl?'

Pearl jumped out of her daydreams with a start. 'Oh – nothing – just looking at the stars,' she stammered.

Amber was lighting a little oil lamp; it seemed strange to Pearl, sitting at the table where she and Mum had eaten all their meals. But Amber was good company, and it was cosy in the warm, golden circle of lamplight.

'That was terrific, Pearl!' Amber mopped up the last bit of egg with her bread. 'Who taught you to cook like that?'

'Mum of course. I always liked helping her, and then when she…when she wasn't too good, sometimes I did all the cooking.'

'I see.' Amber looked thoughtful.

'But I liked doing it, honestly.' Pearl didn't want Amber to get the wrong impression. She hobbled over to the rocking chair, and picked up a little packet wrapped in tissue paper. 'I made this for you.' Shyly she gave the necklace to Amber.

Amber unwrapped her present. 'Why, Pearl, that's really lovely!' She smiled with pleasure. 'You really do have a lot of talents!'

She put the necklace on. In the lamplight the gold beads glowed against her dark skin. Pearl showed Amber the bracelet she had made for herself, and the necklace for Mum.

'I guess you're artistic, like your mum,' said Amber,

running the jewellery gently through her fingers.

'How do you know my mum is artistic?' Pearl was surprised.

'Because of all this!' Amber waved her hands at the saloon all around them. 'Those gorgeous peacock cushions, that stained glass hanging, the curtains…all of it. I knew somebody truly artistic had lived on this boat, and made it beautiful.'

'That's what my mum's like,' said Pearl eagerly. 'When she's well, she's the most most brilliant person you could imagine! She painted the little tree on the boat, you know, and all the castles and roses.'

Amber nodded. 'She must have been really great, Pearl.'

'Is really great,' said Pearl fiercely. 'She still is great – it's just that she's been poorly for a long time…'

'Of course she is, Pearl.' Amber quietly cleared the table. 'Now, how about me fixing up your hair for you?'

Pearl sat comfortably at the little table, while Amber got out all her hairdressing equipment.

And soon she was oiling and combing, and plaiting the extensions into Pearl's hair. Her fingers were deft and sensitive, and she didn't hurt one little bit. And while she worked they talked.

'How come you're so good at hairdressing, Amber?'

Amber laughed. 'It's just one of the things I've done along the way, Pearl – along with my artwork.'

'You're an artist?'

'Uh huh. I illustrate children's books.'

Pearl was so astonished she forgot to keep her head still. 'What – *real* books, books you buy in the shops?'

'That's right Pearl. Mostly I illustrate picture books, but sometimes I work on paperbacks for older children, or things like anthologies of poetry.'

For a moment words failed Pearl.

'Wow – I've never met a real artist before, Amber!' she croaked.

'You have,' said Amber quietly. 'Your mother is a real artist, and so are you. The only difference is I've had some training.'

'But how – how did you get to be a real artist, when your mum stuck you in a Children's Home like that!'

Then Amber laughed.

'It's a long story, Pearl. And I've had enough questions for today! There – you're finished!'

Amber went into the bathroom and brought out the big mirror. She held it up for Pearl.

Pearl stared at the face in the mirror. A film star gazed back at her, her dark gold hair rippling in the lamplight. Cunningly twisted into her own hair, the extensions gleamed green and silver, and here and there bright, burning copper. Her dark green eyes sparkled with emerald fire.

'That's not me!' she said in disbelief.

'Well, it's certainly not me, and I don't *think* it's Tiggy!'

Pearl burst out laughing. 'I like you, Amber, I really do!' she said.

And for the first time in a long while, the hard knots of anxiety and sadness in her stomach relaxed, and she felt safe and warm, and happy.

Chapter 12

'Roo *croo* croo, roo *croo* croo!'

Pearl stretched sleepily. It was the dove, of course; she drifted back to a warm, spring morning, when she was very little.

'What's he saying, Mum, that bird?'

And Mum had said, 'I *love* you, I *love* you, of course!'

There, as always, curled tightly in her arms, Tiggy was purring blissfully. For a few seconds it seemed as if the clock had turned back, and that the busy rattling coming from the kitchen was the sound of Mum, preparing breakfast.

Then she remembered, and for a few moments disappointment and loss swept through her.

Of course – it was Amber who was in the kitchen. And today was the second day of her journey back to Mum.

She pulled back the bluebird curtains. Sunlight streamed into the cabin, and through the crystal hanging in front of her window. A shower of rainbows danced around the walls, and fluttered on her skin.

Rainbows.

Pearl remembered how Mum had once told her the story of Noah's Ark when she was little. How, after the terrible flood, God had promised Noah that He wouldn't ever get so angry with people again, and that He would send them a rainbow in the sky, to show them that He would always protect them.

It was a promise from God, Mum said.

Promises.

Promises that must never be broken.

Pearl tapped the little crystal, and watched the rainbows leap and spin around the room. Suddenly she felt strong, and glad. She slipped down from her bunk, and put her foot cautiously on the floor.

It hardly hurt at all.

She folded back the cabin doors.

'Hi – did you sleep well?' Amber was busy in the galley. A delicious smell of coffee and toast drifted towards her. 'I thought it was my turn to cook! Do you like waffles?'

'After scotch pancakes, waffles are my next best thing!'

Pearl sat down in her rocking chair. It was so good to wake up in the morning and know everything was all right – to find breakfast all ready for her, and Amber calm and smiling in the galley. No worries about whether there was enough food to eat; no Mum still in bed, sick

91

and crying. Pearl felt a pang of remorse.

How could she even think like that?

It wasn't Mum's fault she felt so bad in the mornings – she was ill! Still, it *was* nice not to have to worry. It was lovely to be looked after.

After a quick shower and breakfast, Pearl and Amber sat around the table making plans.

'The first thing we must do, Pearl, is to buy you some more clothes – you really can't go on wearing those!'

Pearl felt a bit embarrassed. 'I haven't got much money, Amber.'

'That doesn't matter – if you'll let me, I'd love to buy you a few things.'

Pearl nodded, gratefully.

'There's a little shopping centre at Willoughby,' said Amber. 'It won't be Top Shop, but there's a place there that sells everything except the kitchen sink. I'm afraid you can't come, though, Pearl – it's too much of a risk.'

Pearl knew Amber was right, but she was so tired of being indoors all the time. Still – only one more day, and she would be with Mum, and as free as a bird!

Amber took the boat the few miles to Willoughby, while Pearl washed up and tidied the cabin.

'Right, Pearl.' Amber looked at Pearl seriously. 'I'll only be gone about half an hour; promise me you'll stay below deck.'

'I promise.'

'Great – I should have some nice surprises for you when I get back!'

Pearl watched forlornly as Amber strode off along the towpath.

It seemed very quiet on the boat. For a moment she longed to open the doors and peep outside. Perhaps she could just go up on deck for a moment – it was so quiet, surely no one would see her?

Then she remembered her promise and sighed.

Amber had left her a big drawing pad and some very classy art crayons. *I know – I'll draw Tiggy*, she thought. She had just started to colour in Tiggy's eyes, when she felt the boat wobble as Amber leaped aboard.

'Right! I hope you like these!' Amber placed a large shopping bag in front of Pearl. 'There wasn't a lot of choice, I'm afraid.'

Pearl rifled in the bag.

Three pairs of briefs – really pretty – three matching camis, in lilac, pink and white, four pairs of socks, two T-shirts, a pair of jeans, and some soft cotton shorts and tops for night-time.

The T-shirts and jeans were really cool.

'Thanks, Amber,' said Pearl. 'They're brill!'

'And here's something to help you pass the time.' Amber gave Pearl a paper bag with something heavy inside it.

'A book!'

Pearl opened the book carefully. It had bright, glowing illustrations.

Then she turned back to the cover.

The Tiger Book of Girls Stories said the title.

And underneath: *Illustrated by Amber Jacobs*

'It's by you – it's got your illustrations!' cried Pearl.

Amber smiled. 'That's right. Usually I have some spare copies hanging around, but I was right out and then I saw this in the newsagents!'

Pearl hugged the book tightly to her chest. She felt her cheeks glow warm. 'Thank you very much,' she said, shyly. She swallowed hard – no one except her mum had ever given her a book before.

'I'm glad you like it, love.' And Amber gave her nose a quick rub.

Somehow the day sped by.

They made excellent time all the way down the Grand Union Canal, and by late afternoon were only about ten miles from Broughton.

'Time to find a mooring place for the night!' Amber jumped down into the saloon.

'Couldn't we keep going a bit longer?' pleaded Pearl.

'Sorry Pearl, it's just not safe to travel in the dark. Too many hazards.'

Pearl knew this in her heart, but it was awful to be so near, and yet so far.

'But I promise we'll get started at very first light,' said Amber. 'And we should make Broughton by about nine or ten in the morning. I tell you what – how about you coming up on deck for a bit when it's dark; no one's going to see you then!'

They found a quiet spot near a bank of willows. In the late afternoon sun the branches glowed golden red. Pearl longed to paint them.

Straight after tea – jacket potatoes and sausages cooked by Pearl – Amber carried two little folding chairs onto the rear deck.

'OK, come on out!' she called.

It was wonderful to feel the clean, fresh air on her face. Pearl breathed in deeply, savouring the smells of grass and water, and somewhere a hint of wood smoke on the wind.

Amber gave her a blanket, for the night was cold. 'Going to be a frost tonight, Pearl. You can always tell when the stars are this bright.'

Pearl nodded.

Silence enfolded them like a blessing. Overhead arched the heavens, vast, majestic, brilliant. A million, million stars blazed down on her.

Millions and billions, thought Pearl, *on and on forever*. Suddenly she felt really small.

Was God really up there, beyond the stars?

Did anyone really care what happened to her?

She thought of the rainbow and the Noah story.

95

Her mother's gentle voice echoed in her ears. She felt her warm arms encircling her, could even smell the scent of roses and bread that was her mother.

And a wonderful sense of peace and calm entered her, and she knew that somehow, in the end, everything was going to be all right.

Chapter 13

'Come on, Pearl – you must eat something!' Amber's voice jolted Pearl out of her dreams.

'I'm sorry – I'm just not hungry!' Pearl pushed the bowl of cereal away from her. 'My stomach's closed down, Amber!'

'Too excited – is that it?'

Pearl nodded. 'I just want to get going – only three more hours, and we'll be at Broughton!'

Pearl imagined them gliding into the marina – past the crowds of other boats, and down the canal to the quiet stretch where the golden elderberry arched over the water…and there would be Mum, waiting for her, happy and smiling, her copper hair streaming in the breeze…

She had played this scene in her mind so many times – last thing before she went to sleep, in the early hours of the morning when she was wide awake with excitement, while she washed and dressed.

'Well, if you can't eat, at least drink up your juice!'

'Sorry, Amber.' Pearl shook herself awake and gulped down her orange juice in one go.

'OK Pearl!' Amber laughed. 'You'll do. Suppose you clear away, while I get us going?'

Pearl rushed around the saloon, clearing the breakfast pots, washing Tiggy's little silver bowl, wiping down the table. It was a huge relief to be doing something. Up on deck she heard Amber start the engine. The familiar throbbing calmed and steadied her.

She drew back the curtains. Outside it was only just light. As the sun struck the water, a million little stars flickered into life. Amber had been right about the frost; on the canal banks, the reeds were feathered with glittering crystals, and looping the long grasses, spiders' webs made a fairyland of iced lace.

Pearl grabbed her drawing book, and tried to capture what she saw. It was difficult – so difficult that for a while she relaxed, and forgot to fret.

When she glanced at the clock it said half past eight.

They had had been going for over an hour; Amber must be freezing up there in the icy cold. Pearl put the kettle on, and made two mugs of hot chocolate.

'Amber!' She stuck her head cautiously through the cabin doors. 'I've made you a hot drink.'

There was no one about. She looked wistfully at Amber.

'All right – you can come out for a few minutes.'

It was so good to be out in the fresh air. Pearl looked all around her.

'I know where we are. That's Withybrook over there. That means we're going through the big tunnel at Thornton soon!'

'Uh huh – in about twenty minutes, I reckon. And then it should only take us another hour to reach Broughton,' Amber smiled.

Pearl saw something moving on the canal bank, way ahead. In the distance, dogs barked.

'Early morning walkers, Pearl – you get below deck straightaway!'

Pearl didn't need telling twice. How awful if someone spotted her, so near to finding her mother.

She drew the curtains, and settled down in the saloon. She flipped through the book Amber had bought her. Some of the stories looked really good, and Amber's illustrations were truly brilliant.

One day, I'll ask her to teach me how to draw like that, thought Pearl.

But of course – after today, she wouldn't be seeing Amber again. Somehow the thought shocked her, and for a little while she felt sad.

It struck her how much she liked Amber. She was a grown up, but a real friend. A bit like an older sister, perhaps – or an aunty. Pearl had sometimes wished she had more people in her family. Once there had been Nanna, but after she had died...

This wouldn't do!

Pearl opened the book at a promising story and tried to read. She read the same sentence three times, but somehow it wouldn't go in. She pushed the book away and went into the bathroom. For the third time that day, Pearl re-arranged her hair. Would Mum recognise her, with her new hairstyle?

Of course she would!

Pearl looked at herself critically. She had put on her new jeans, and her favourite T-shirt; yes, she felt good in them – they were cool, dead cool.

She wanted to look her very best for Mum.

She drifted back into the saloon, and looked at the clock.

A quarter to nine.

Pearl sighed. How slowly the time was passing. What could she do, to make it go more quickly?

Then she remembered the poem she had sent in the letter to her Mum. She could write it out again, and decorate it really beautifully.

Pearl copied the poem carefully. She enclosed it as she had done before in a golden ring. Then she wove a circlet of flowers all around the ring, and coloured them – wild roses, buttercups, and tiny blue violets...

She lost all sense of time; the world outside darkened, the lights in the cabin came on, but Pearl didn't notice.

Now what should she do? How about doing another word poem for Mum! Which word should she choose this time?

Then it came to her – she would do Mum's name! Carefully she wrote:

M
E
L
I
S
S
A

For a long time she scribbled and crossed out. This was hard – much harder than her first poem. But finally she had it:

M um I miss you so much
E very day I think about you
L ove you more than I can say
I n my heart for ever
S ome day we'll meet again
S oon I'll hold you in my arms
A ll I want is you

*

Pearl gave a deep sigh of satisfaction She outlined the initial letters of Mum's name in gold. Then she drew a large pink heart around the poem, and coloured it in.

'Pearl!' Amber's face peered around the cabin door. 'Did you enjoy the tunnel?'

They'd been through the tunnel and she hadn't realised!

Amber laughed at the startled expression on Pearl's face. 'You don't mean to say you didn't notice, you dozy date!'

'I've been busy…writing something special for Mum.' Pearl felt herself blushing. She pushed the poems under the drawing pad; somehow she didn't want Amber to see them. Some things were private.

'I guess it must have been something really special, Pearl,' said Amber gently. 'Another twenty minutes or so, and we'll be there, you know.'

Twenty minutes! That was no time at all!

'But you'll have to keep out of sight, Pearl – sorry. Why don't you sit on the window seat, and peep through the curtains?'

Oh, such a slow twenty minutes!

Pearl peered through the peacock curtains, noticing every familiar little landmark.

There was the little bridge about a mile from the marina. Now they were through it, and gliding down the final stretch. There was the long bank of willows, and there the tumbledown farm with the crooked chimneys.

Any minute now…

Pearl jiggled up and down. Her feet wouldn't keeps still, and her hands were pressing hard against the windows, willing the boat on, faster, faster.

And there, suddenly, was the wide basin of the marina, the brightly painted boats gleaming in the winter sunshine. Columns of smoke rose from some chimneys. There were very few people about.

Pearl strained her eyes, scanning the boats. She recognised the names of all those moored in the basin; there were no new boats. But then, they never moored in that part of the marina.

No – her mother would be where they always stayed, underneath the elderberry tree…

They glided past the little shop that sold everything under the sun, past the boat repair yard, and down the quiet stretch beyond.

Suddenly the engine switched off, and Amber appeared at the cabin doors. 'Is this the stretch where you usually moor the boat?'

Pearl nodded. 'A little bit further down there, by the magic…by the little elderberry tree.'

Slowly, oh so slowly, Amber took the boat those final few metres.

And there was the elderberry tree – stark in its winter nakedness.

And that was it.

No new boat.

No Mum.

Pearl felt numb with shock.

She had been so *sure* Mum would be here. She had seen it so often in her mind…

Amber slipped quietly down the cabin steps.

'Maybe she's somewhere in the marina, Pearl…in the shop perhaps—'

That was it!

Of course, she wouldn't be sitting there on the bank, in winter, not if she hadn't bought the new boat yet. She'd be in the shop, or the little cafe, having a hot drink.

'Will you look for me, Amber, please?'

'Of course I will, sweetheart.' Amber's face was creased with concern. 'You stay here, and I'll have a really good look round.'

Very carefully, Pearl described her mother.

'I'll be as quick as I can,' said Amber. 'Now, promise me you'll stay on the boat?'

'I promise!'

Amber vaulted over the side of the boat, and backtracked to the marina.

Pearl watched her until she turned a bend in the canal and out of sight.

Silence.

She felt her hands go icy cold and sweaty. She started to shiver. She huddled closer to the stove. How long was the silence – how long!

And then, footsteps along the tow path...

Pearl couldn't help herself. She ran up the cabin steps, and scrambled over the side of the boat.

Amber was walking towards her.

Alone.

'I'm sorry, sweetheart; I've combed every bit of the marina – asked questions – she's not here, Pearl—'

The sun went black in Pearl's eyes, and the world began to spin.

Chapter 14

'Pearl, I've made you a cup of hot chocolate; come on, sweetheart, sit up and have a drink – it'll make you feel better.'

Silence.

Amber looked at the prickly little body on the bed, tightly curled like a frightened hedgehog, and sighed. An hour had passed since the awful realisation that her mother was not there, and most probably wasn't even looking for her. It had struck Pearl like a blow. Amber had helped Pearl inside, placed her safely on her bed, and warmed her icy hands and feet.

Now Amber tried for the third time to get Pearl to sit up and have a drink – to talk, to cry – anything rather than this frozen silence.

But Pearl had simply curled into an even tighter ball, and turned her face to the wall of the boat. Sighing, Amber placed the hot chocolate on Pearl's bedside table, and walked quietly into the kitchen.

Time passed, and still Pearl did not stir.

In the saloon, Tiggy sat washing her face.

Something was wrong – and Tiggy knew it as surely as she had known where her heart and home lay, when she found her way back, across roads and rivers to the boat.

She trotted briskly into Pearl's cabin, and leaped up onto her bunk.

She sniffed Pearl delicately, drawing in the powerful sense of loss and despair. Then sweetly, gently, as a mother cat warms its kitten, she washed Pearl's face.

And as the rough, warm little tongue caressed her, Pearl felt something hard inside her melt and dissolve, and then the tears began to flow. Pearl cried and cried, while Tiggy gently mopped up her tears. Then she reached out her arms and held Tiggy close.

In the saloon, Amber heard the sounds of weeping, and wisely left Pearl in Tiggy's care. And when the sobbing finally ceased, she came into Pearl's cabin and sat quietly on the bed.

Gently she stroked Pearl's hair.

Pearl struggled to sit up.

And suddenly she wanted to talk. 'Where is she, Amber? Why hasn't she come to get me? I was so *sure* she would be here. I've looked and looked for her, all the places where she would come…if she was looking for me.' Pearl took a paper hanky from Amber and blew her nose. 'What did she run away for, if she wasn't coming to get me?'

Amber sighed deeply. 'I wish I knew the answer, Pearl…but I don't.'

'If I'd lost my daughter,' said Pearl in a shaky voice, 'I would look and look until I found her. Why hasn't she come, Amber, why?'

All of a sudden Pearl was angry. 'I hate her! I hate her! She's not a proper mother. A proper mother would have come and got me!' She thumped her pillow furiously.

Amber didn't say anything. She didn't say Pearl was wrong to say that about her mother. She just sat and waited until Pearl had calmed down. Then she went into the saloon and put the kettle on.

A few minutes later, Pearl sat in the rocking chair, sipping a cup of hot chocolate.

It was strange.

Something really awful should have happened to her, because of what she had said about Mum.

But it hadn't.

Strangely, she felt much calmer – almost peaceful. 'Amber – did you ever feel you hated your mum?'

'Oh Pearl, yes – lots of times! When she stuck me in that Children's Home, so she could be with her boyfriend, I hated her so much!'

'But your mum was a horrible mum – no wonder you hated her! My mum – my mum wasn't like that—'

'No, she wasn't Pearl, but she's not here for you now when you need her…you must feel as if she doesn't want you – as if she can't be bothered—'

Pearl nodded. 'She never wrote back to me, Amber, not once – and I sent her lots of letters and wrote her a special poem—'

Suddenly Pearl wanted to show Amber the poems she had done for Mum – both of them. She picked up her sketch book and handed it silently to Amber.

For a long while Amber looked at the poems.

'Pearl, these are beautiful poems. Thank you very much for letting me see them.'

Pearl took the poems back and looked at them in silence.

'You know, Pearl – when you write about your mum, it's as if she was so perfect; was she really like that all the time?'

Pearl took a deep breath, and shook her head. 'My mum – when she was well, she was the best mum in all the world, but—'

'But when she was ill…?'

'When she was ill it was like she was another person. She used to get so angry – and sometimes she used to go around the boat smashing things up, and shouting—'

'Did she ever hit you, Pearl?' asked Amber quietly.

'She used to throw things at me sometimes…when she was really upset, but then she was always so sorry afterwards—' Pearl's voice shook at the memory. 'And then after that, she would go to the shops, and buy cans and cans of cider, and drink and drink, and then she would be so sick the next day…and then she would lie in bed and sleep for days, and not get up—'

'And who looked after her when she was like that?'

'I did,' said Pearl in a very small voice. 'I didn't really mind, because I loved her so much, but sometimes, it felt scary, and I wished I didn't have to be the grown up…'

Amber squeezed Pearl's hand.

'And then she would get better, and be happy again, and she would be so much fun, and she'd dance and play with me, and buy me things, and we'd have such a lovely time—'

'It must have been very hard Pearl – very confusing.'

Pearl nodded. 'It was like she was two people, Amber, a nice one, and a nasty one. You know that rhyme about the little girl with a curl?'

Amber smiled.

> *'There was a little girl,*
> *And she had a little curl,*
> *Right in the middle of her forehead;*
> *And when she was good,*
> *She was very very good,*
> *And when she was bad*
> *She was horrid!'*

'That's it!' said Pearl 'That's just it...she was like that little girl.'

'Only she wasn't a little girl, she was your mum,' said Amber quietly. 'Was she always like this, Pearl?'

Pearl shook her head. 'No – it started after Nanna died, that's what brought it on. She saw the doctor at first, and he gave her some pills, but she wouldn't take them – she said they made her feel like a zombie.'

'Pearl, I think what you've told me shows that your mother was very sick, in her mind, and that's why she had to go to hospital. I think it's possible she's so sick that she's not sure what she's doing – she's confused – and that's why she ran away.'

Pearl nodded silently.

'And it doesn't mean she doesn't love you, Pearl, it's just that she's very sick and needs treatment.'

'So…maybe she's lost and doesn't know what she's doing?'

'Maybe. But at least you know your mother loves you, Pearl. Now mine – she just didn't give a monkey's about me!'

Pearl smiled weakly at Amber. 'She must have been really stupid, then. I'd have loved you, if you'd been my little girl!'

'Hmm.' Amber sniffed and wiped her nose. 'Look Pearl – I haven't suggested this to you before now, because you were so sure you were going to find your mum, but why don't we put the telly on, and see if there's anything about you and your mum on the news?'

'You've got a telly?' Pearl had wondered what had happened to the old television set.

'Yes – in my cabin; to encourage me not to watch it too often! In fact, I don't put it on much these days – too much rubbish – but we could switch it on for the one o'clock news.'

At two minutes to one, Pearl sat on Amber's bunk, waiting for the news.

The headlines were full of bombs and terrorists as usual. Then came the regional news. There was a feature about a man who'd been mugged in the centre of Nottingham, and then the presenter looked grave, and said, 'Police are still searching for the missing schoolgirl, Pearl Lovett.'

A photo of Pearl appeared on the screen. Pearl gasped and clapped her hands over her mouth. How strange to see herself on telly like that!

'Since early sightings in Boxton in Leicestershire, Pearl seems to have disappeared. The search has now switched to Birmingham, to the area around Beechwood Hospital where Pearl's mother, Melissa Lovett, was recently a patient. It is thought Pearl might be trying to find her mother, who went missing from Beechwood the day before Pearl's disappearance.'

Then suddenly, there was Bernie, on the screen, talking about Pearl.

And then Jenny.

Their faces looked grey and sad...

Amber switched off the television.

There was a long silence.

Then Amber looked deep into Pearl's eyes, and said, 'Pearl, do you remember your promise to me? Before we set out for Broughton?'

Pearl nodded.

'I think the time has come for me to phone the police, Pearl, and tell them you're safe.'

Pearl twisted her hands together miserably. Yes, it was true, she had promised. And Jenny and Bernie had looked so sad. She'd been trying to shut them out of her mind...

But oh, she didn't want to go back...to have to face everyone at school about the stolen books, to see the expressions of disappointment and dislike on everyone's face. Besides, Jenny might say she wouldn't have her anymore, and she would have to go into a Home...

And most of all, she didn't want to leave the boat – her home – and Amber.

And Tiggy.

Above all, Tiggy.

She remembered something she'd seen on the television, before the news came on; all those glittering lights, and dancing snowmen – and Rudolph, and a jolly

Father Christmas. 'Amber? What's the date?'

Amber smiled wryly. 'I was wondering when you'd ask! It's December the twenty third.'

'December the...it's two days before Christmas!'

'That's right, Pearl.' Amber sighed.

A hundred memories flashed into Pearl's mind. Happy Christmases, Mum full of fun, making mince pies...both of them making paper chains to decorate the boat...secrets everywhere, hidden parcels, stockings...

And unhappy Christmases, Mum sick in bed, and Pearl trying to cheer her up...

She switched off that memory quickly. But always, always, Christmas on the boat...

Pearl looked up, straight into Amber's eyes. 'Amber, I promise, I solemnly promise, that if you will let me stay on the boat for Christmas, I'll...I'll let you phone Jenny, and everyone...only I couldn't bear it, to go back now, and leave Tiggy, and everything...at Christmas.'

Amber sighed deeply. 'You do realise that I'm going to be in *really* big trouble about this, Pearl? I mean, I could even be accused of kidnapping, you know!'

'But you didn't kidnap me, Amber! You – you rescued me! I'll tell everyone, you'll see...I won't let you get into trouble.'

For a moment Amber stared hard at her feet.

She thought about being ten, and alone in a Children's Home for Christmas.

The Christmas her mum had been too busy to send her a present, or even a card.

She looked up at Pearl and smiled. 'OK Pearl, you win.'

Pearl leaped out of her chair and threw her arms around Amber.

'Oh thank you, thank you, thank you, Amber! I'll be so good, honest, you won't be sorry.'

'Will you get off me you banana, you're standing on my foot!' gasped Amber.

But she was smiling and rubbing her nose, and Pearl knew she was pleased.

Chapter 15

'Right – I won't be long, Pearl – just long enough to do a spot of Christmas shopping!'

It was Christmas Eve; Amber picked up a huge shopping bag, and put on her warm padded jacket.

Pearl sighed. 'I don't suppose—?'

'You don't suppose right, Pearl. There's no way you can come with me – you'd be spotted straightaway! But I'll be back very soon. Why don't you have a look see if you can find any Christmas decorations?'

Pearl brightened – of course, if Amber had kept the boat just as it used to be, then she knew exactly where to find them.

Amber waved at Pearl through the saloon windows, and strode off down the towpath towards Broughton. And as she walked, a conversation took place in her head.

'*You are a bigger fool that I thought you were, Amber Jacobs,*' said the Voice of Common Sense.

'I know, I know,' sighed Amber. 'I was going to have a lovely, peaceful time – a little holiday for a week or two, before I get stuck into the next book…'

'*Yes, and now look at what you've done!*' accused Common Sense. '*Got yourself lumbered with a kid for Christmas! And you were going to invite Annie and Liz for a few days; so that plan's right down the pan! And besides – do you realise you're going to be in really big trouble with the law!*'

'Wouldn't be the first time,' said Amber, remembering the many times she had run away as a child.

'*But you're not a child, now, are you?*' said Common Sense. '*You should know better!*'

'All right, all right!' said Amber. 'I've made a promise – as soon as Christmas is over, I'll do the sensible thing!'

And she shoved her hands into her pockets, gave her head a shake, and silenced Common Sense once and for all.

Yes, she was a fool.

But she wasn't going to let that child go back to heaven-knows-what for Christmas. She'd had too many Christmases in Care herself for that.

'At least I can give her a Christmas to remember,' she said aloud, startling a man walking his dog very much indeed.

Amber did a thorough shop in Broughton.

The village Co-op (open all hours) supplied a chicken; sage and onion stuffing; potatoes; carrots; broccoli and peas; as well as a Christmas pudding you could microwave;

a dozen extra special mince pies; a chocolate log with a robin on top; salad; cold ham; a quiche; mini pizzas; two bottles of coke and everything you need for making a trifle.

She also bought half a kilo of shiny red apples, some satsumas wrapped in gold paper, some grapes, and a bunch of bananas.

Then she staggered along the main street until she reached Broughton Bargain Centre.

It was packed with Christmas shoppers, looking for those little Christmas extras. Amber bought red and gold wrapping paper, a box of Christmas crackers, and lots of mysterious little things. *She's going to have a proper Christmas stocking, too!* thought Amber.

Finally she bought several packets of crisps, some crystalised oranges and lemons, a box of chocolates, and a large chocolate Father Christmas.

'All done and dusted!' said Amber to herself, as she staggered back along the towpath. 'Christmas is well and truly on its way.'

When she reached the boat, Pearl was in a high state of excitement. She'd found the Christmas decorations box, and something else too.

'Look Amber! I've found the boat lights!' Pearl held up a huge loop of cable, along which hung little coloured lanterns. 'And I've tested them – and they work!'

Pearl switched the lights on and the rainbow of

lanterns glowed brightly in the dim saloon.

'Fabulous!' cried Amber. 'We'll do them as soon as I've unpacked the shopping.'

They worked together, stowing away the food.

'Oh – chocolate log! I *adore* chocolate log!' cried Pearl. 'And mince pies too!'

'This is going to be a Christmas to remember, girl,' laughed Amber.

But there were some bags Amber whipped out of Pearl's hands before she could even peer inside. 'Oh no you don't!' Amber said 'No peeping!' And she whisked the bags off into her cabin.

Pearl gave a little shiver of anticipation; this was how Christmas should be. But for a moment a wave of sadness swept over her.

It would be her first Christmas ever apart from her mum.

She took a deep breath. 'But at least I'm in my own home, and with Tiggy,' she whispered to herself. She shook away the dark thoughts, and heaped the fruit bowl with shiny red apples, gleaming satsumas, and golden bananas.

She polished the apple skins till they glowed, then took a piece of tinsel from the decorations box, and wound it round the fruit.

'Brilliant, Pearl!' Amber stood in the doorway admiring Pearl's arrangement. 'But I think before we do anything else, we should move away from Broughton. There are far too many people around.'

'We could go on down the canal towards Little Weeping,' said Pearl. 'There's a really quiet stretch there just before the locks.'

Amber left Pearl alone with the decorations while she steered the boat the three miles to Little Weeping.

It was lunch time when they reached the mooring place. Pearl made some ham and tomato sandwiches for them, and they munched companionably, side by side, in the saloon. Outside, the day was surprisingly warm for December.

'It should snow, for a proper Christmas,' said Pearl.

'But it never does!' they said in unison, and burst out laughing.

It was so quiet along the canal banks, that Amber said Pearl could help string up the lights. It was wonderful to be outside again. Pearl took great gulps of clean country air. In a field nearby two magpies bounced and chattered in a tall ash tree.

'One for sorrow, two for joy...' recited Pearl.

Amber gave her a sudden warm smile, that made her feel glad inside.

Then they switched on the lights and it was Christmas.

All that afternoon Pearl helped Amber put up the decorations. For a moment it hurt when she took out a string of paper chains that she had made when she was really little, with Mum. They had cut up old magazines, and glued them together with flour and water paste...

But Tiggy leaped on the chains and rolled over and over, thrashing them with her hind legs. And in the mad scramble to save the paper chains, she and Amber ended up breathless with laughter.

'She's always like this at Christmas!' gasped Pearl. 'You have to be into everything, don't you, Tiggy!' She found an unbreakable tree decoration and rolled it for Tiggy to chase.

Then Pearl had a thought. 'Amber, we haven't got a Christmas tree!'

'No more we haven't!' exclaimed Amber, her face falling. Then she brightened. 'Tell you what, let's see if we can find a branch off a tree – that will do just as well.'

And because it was Christmas, and no one was around, she let Pearl come out onto the bank to search with her.

They scrambled under the barbed wire into a neighbouring field. Pearl searched the verges, looking for a broken branch. The field went into a little spinney and there, lying on the floor, half buried under a layer of dusty brown leaves, Pearl found the perfect branch – a piece off an oak tree, wonderfully twisty and bent. They carried it back triumphantly to the boat.

Amber's pockets were stuffed to bursting with pine cones she had found, and a little branch of blue fir, smelling so fresh and spicy.

Pearl spent a blissful afternoon working on the oak

branch with Amber. First they blew off all the dust and cobwebs. Then they painted it white. When it was dry, Amber produced some glue, and a packet of silver stardust. Carefully, carefully, Pearl streaked the glue along the branches.

Next came the fun bit; they took the branch outside, and Pearl scattered stardust all over it. And suddenly, it was a little tree, glittering, magical.

Then a flurry of wind swept some of the stardust into the canal, and Pearl watched, fascinated, as a galaxy of stars spun in ever-increasing circles on the water.

Amber took an empty flower pot from the trough on the roof of the boat, and filled it with earth. She pushed the little tree into the pot, and firmed it down until it stood up strong and secure, then weighed it down with pebbles from the bank.

They stood the tree in the corner of the saloon. Pearl hung it with silver and blue baubles, and twisted the white fairy lights around the branches. On the topmost branch she placed the little glass angel. Then she switched on the lights, and the saloon became a fairyland. High on the top of the tree, the angel's wings glimmered with blue fire.

Pearl shivered with pleasure. For a moment or two she gazed silently at the little angel. Could you make wishes to angels?

Pearl took a deep breath, and closed her eyes tightly.

She made a wish, a secret wish, and blew it gently to the top of the tree.

It was getting dark outside. Now Amber was very busy shut away in her cabin. Tantalising rustling noises, the shirr of scissors, and the crackling of paper reached Pearl's ears.

She had a sudden thought; she hadn't got a Christmas present for Amber! But how could she give Amber a present when she couldn't go shopping?

Pearl racked her brains. Then very quietly she slipped outside onto the canal bank. The light was fading fast, but she could just about see. She searched the hedgerows, scissors in hand. Her arms full, she crept silently back onto the boat.

Quickly she set to work. She found a baking potato and cut it in half. She sliced a bit off one side, and stood it on an old enamel plate. Snipping away, she cut little twigs of scarlet – berried holly and stuck them into the potato. Here and there she wove fragrant branches of fir. Then she coiled ivy all around the edges of the plate, so that you couldn't see the old plate or the potato.

She chose some tiny silver and gold baubles from the box of Christmas decorations, and set them amongst the dark, shiny leaves. Finally, she pushed a snow-white candle right into the centre of the potato, so it stood up straight and tall.

Good! That was one present made!

Pearl tiptoed into her cabin, and wrapped Amber's present in tissue paper.

Now – what else could she do?

Of course – she could write a special poem for her!

Pearl took out her sketch pad, and the coloured pencils Amber had given her. On a clean sheet of paper, she wrote:

A
M
B
E
R

For a long time she scribbled and crossed out and scribbled again. It was so hard to get something just right!

At last, she was satisfied. Carefully she copied the poem right into the centre of a clean page. It said:

A lways there when you need her
M y new special friend
B eautiful and strong
E ver kind and true
R escued me when I was lost

She coloured the capitals carefully with golds, and reds and oranges. And all around she drew a garland of autumn leaves in glowing amber colours.

There!

She was just in time – she could hear Amber clearing up next door. Quickly she wrapped her work in dark gold tissue paper, and tied it with curly red ribbon.

'You've been very quiet!' said Amber, a mischievous twinkle in her eye. 'What have you been up to?'

'Aha – that would be telling!' laughed Pearl. Then she had a thought. 'Oh my goodness, I haven't got a present for Tiggy!'

'All Tiggy will want on Christmas day is her share of the chicken!' said Amber.

'But I always give her something,' said Pearl in dismay.

'How about something to play with?' suggested Amber.

'Good idea!' said Pearl 'I know!'

She ferreted about in the old needlework box, and pulled out a length of thin elastic. She found a slender branch they had cut off the little Christmas tree, and tied one end of the elastic securely round the top. Then she made a pompom from scraps of old wool, and tied it onto the elastic.

'There!' she said. 'A Tiggy Teaser!' And she bounced it up and down.

'I should put that away quick,' said Amber. 'Tiggy's looking very interested right now!'

Pearl wrapped up the Tiggy Teaser, and squirelled it away in her cabin. Good – now she was ready for Christmas!

After a quick makeshift tea, Amber busied herself in the kitchen with the trifle. 'Why don't you switch on the telly?' she called. 'I think you'll find *The Wizard of Oz* starts in about fifteen minutes.'

The Wizard of Oz!

Pearl was in raptures. She'd watched it every Christmas at Nanna's for as long as she could remember.

They spent the evening curled up on Amber's bed, watching the old story of Dorothy and Toto. And they sang along with all the songs.

'I love the munchkins, don't you?' said Pearl.

'Mmm – but I think the Cowardly Lion is my very favourite character – and I love the Tin Man.'

As she watched Dorothy's adventures, Pearl's heart began to beat fast. And at the end, it was hard not to get weepy, when Dorothy so wanted to get home.

She's like me, thought Pearl. *Just like me.*

When the film had finished Amber opened the box of crystalised fruit, and they ate their way though the whole lot.

'I think I want to go to bed now,' said Pearl. 'It'll make the morning come quicker!'

That night, tucked up safely in her bunk with Tiggy, Pearl fell into a deep and dreamless sleep.

She didn't hear her cabin door open oh-so-softly at midnight.

And she didn't see Someone tiptoe in and place a large, fat stocking at the the foot of her bed.

Chapter 16

It was the day after Boxing Day. Pearl lay snugly in her bed, cradled by the gentle rocking of boat, and the soft slap-slap of the water against her cabin walls. She was in that pleasant state between sleeping and waking; Tiggy was purring quietly into her left ear, and for a few precious moments her mind flooded with happy memories.

What a Christmas Day it had been! No – not the best ever – that could only be with Mum, but brilliant, dead brilliant. In the morning she had rushed into Amber's cabin to show her 'what Father Christmas had brought.' She had sat on Amber's bunk, pulling out the little gifts one by one...a packet of rainbow beads for making jewellery; a little bottle of frosted silver nail polish; a box of beautiful art crayons all her own; a little notebook with a picture of a tortoiseshell cat on the cover, just like Tiggy; a beautiful comb for her hair; a magnifying glass; a strip of hologram butterfly transfers;

sweets; lollipops; an *enormous* chocolate Father Christmas; and of course, an apple and an orange wrapped in gold paper...so many things.

She had given Amber a big hug, and she knew Amber liked it, even though she said, 'Give over, you banana!' and sniffed and rubbed her nose.

After breakfast they sat round the little Christmas tree, opening their presents. Amber loved her Christmas decoration, and said it must go right in the middle of the table for Christmas dinner. And she had been very pleased with the poem Pearl had written for her.

'I'll get a special frame for that, Pearl, and put it up in my cabin. It's beautiful, really beautiful.'

For a moment Pearl saw Amber's eyes shining very brightly. Then she turned away, and went quickly into the galley.

Then there had been Amber's main present to Pearl. It was a book – a *poetry* book, illustrated by Amber. Pearl looked at the cover, and her heart beat fast...surely she knew that book?

With a start, she realised. It was a copy of the gorgeous anthology she had stolen from the library, that dreadful day. Her cheeks burned, and she was troubled.

'Don't you like it, Pearl?' Amber said gently.

Pearl pushed away the past, with all its guilt and horror. Slowly it dawned on her that this time, the book was really and truly hers.

'Oh Amber, it's lovely,' she whispered. 'No one except Mum has ever given me a book before.'

Pearl looked inside it. Wonderingly, she read:

> To Pearl,
> my special friend,
> with love from Amber

Underneath she had signed it, and written the date.

Pearl had sat for ages, drinking in the poetry and the beautiful illustrations. And there was a box of water-colour paints, and a big sketch book to go with it...and a game, and some poetry magnets for the fridge.

Pearl had spent a long and happy morning with her presents, while Tiggy had a wonderful time leaping on all the wrapping paper, and shredding it to pieces. She loved the Tiggy Teaser! Pearl and Amber laughed as she leaped and twirled after the bouncing pompom, until Pearl took pity on her, and let her catch it, and drum it with her hind legs.

Pearl sighed deeply, and turned over in her bunk, remembering. Then there had been Christmas dinner, with all the trimmings, and a sleepy afternoon when she had curled up with Amber and Tiggy, and watched *Chicken Run*. Afterwards they played with her new game. It involved a lot of drawing and miming. Amber had Pearl in tucks with her funny mimes...

And throughout the day, Amber had taken loads of photos – of Pearl, and of Tiggy, of the Christmas tree, and of Pearl wearing a silly hat for Christmas dinner. Then Pearl took some really lovely snaps of Amber

Slowly Pearl came out of her rosy dream.

She really didn't want to.

But she knew what day it was.

The Day After Boxing Day.

The day when she had to keep her promise to Amber, and let her phone the police.

Amber had been so kind to her. She had let Pearl stay over Boxing Day, and had done everything she could to make it a good last day. She had shown her how to print out her art work from the computer, and they had played with the poetry magnets. Amber had written some very funny poems, but Pearl could only write what was in her heart.

Pearl's poem stood out starkly on the fridge door:

> I do not want to go,
> I do not want to go.
> It's dark outside,
> I do not want to go.

Amber had sighed, and said, 'Oh Pearl,' and given her a big hug.

And now it was time.

Pearl was very suddenly awake. There was a heaviness in her stomach, a great yawning darkness. And there was something else. When she had recovered from the terrible disappointment that her Mum was not at Broughton, and hadn't run away from the hospital to find her, Pearl had felt so angry, so hurt and betrayed, that she had pushed away all thoughts of her mother. She closed a door in her mind, and concentrated on what she had salvaged from the past – Tiggy, dear Tiggy, who had never let her down, and the boat, her beloved home.

And then there had been Amber, and Christmas, bright candles in the darkness...

But now Christmas was over, a nagging thought she had tried so hard to banish filtered back into her mind.

Where was Mum?

Was she OK?

A picture came into Pearl's mind, and she saw her mother curled up in a shop doorway, cold and hungry, like the homeless people she'd seen on telly...

No, not that!

With a huge effort of mind, she pushed the dark thoughts away.

At least if she went back to Jenny's – or to whatever was waiting for her – she would get to hear about her mum as soon as she was found...Bernie would see to that.

Amber stuck her head round the cabin door. 'Hi,

sweetheart – I'm just making breakfast. Could you fancy some Scotch pancakes?'

Pearl shook her head. The lump in her stomach seemed to be moving upwards. She felt sick.

Amber came and sat on the edge of the bed. 'It's hard, Pearl, it's hard…but there's something I want you to know…I'll never forget you, ever.'

Pearl looked straight into Amber's eyes. 'Promise,' she said huskily, 'promise.'

'I promise,' said Amber. And her voice was strong and firm, and Pearl knew she meant it.

'Will you write?' Pearl blinked hard.

'Of course I will – often – and I'll come and see you, too, if they'll let me. And you never know, they might even let you come and stay with me sometimes.'

For a moment hope flickered in the darkness of Pearl's mind. Then a really brilliant idea struck her. 'I know, Amber, you could foster me, and then I could come and live with you – at least until Mum's better!'

Amber smiled sadly. 'Oh Pearl, I don't think anyone would let me foster you, sweetheart…I think they'd say I wasn't a suitable person – not being married, and living on a boat and everything. And I have a feeling I'm going to be in a spot of bother for keeping you here, as well…'

'You didn't keep me, Amber,' said Pearl. 'I wanted to stay here. I begged you!'

'I know,' sighed Amber, 'but still—'

133

'And there's something else, Amber,' said Pearl hesitantly. 'Will you promise to look after Tiggy for me, until I find Mum?'

'Of course I will, Pearl – anyone can see she's your cat. I'll look after her until you're with your mum again. Then you can have her back – honest – cross my heart. Now, come on; get dressed, and see if you can eat just a tiny little bit of breakfast.'

Pearl put on her very best clothes, so that everyone could see how well Amber had looked after her. But she couldn't eat any breakfast at all. She sipped slowly at her mug of hot chocolate.

And then the moment came.

With her arm tightly around Pearl, Amber picked up her mobile, and dialled 999. Pearl heard her say. 'Police, please.'

Then speaking very clearly Amber said, 'I have the missing schoolgirl, Pearl Lovett, here with me…she's very well, and quite safe…'

Amber told the police exactly where the *ELDERFLOWER* was moored, and put the phone down. They sat in silence, Amber holding Pearl's hand tightly. Pearl's knees started to shake, so Amber tucked her up warmly with a rug. The silence seemed to go on forever. Then suddenly, very near, there were footsteps running along the tow path, and a loud knock at the saloon door.

Amber opened the door. 'Please come in,' she said quietly.

Then the world went mad. The first policeman had a dog with him. Tiggy arched her back, hissed loudly, and fled. But the policeman had the dog firmly under control, and told Pearl not to be afraid.

'Gentle as a lamb, he is,' he smiled.

A policewoman came into the saloon, and squatted down by Pearl.

'Hello, Pearl,' she said gently. 'Are you all right?'

Pearl nodded silently, and clung onto Amber's hand. Then the policewoman turned to Amber and starting asking her a lot of questions.

At first they were friendly questions, but when it became clear that Amber had not just found Pearl, but that Pearl had been with her on the boat most of the time she had been missing, the questions grew less friendly, and the policewoman's voice took on a different tone.

'Are you aware, Miss Jacobs, that you have committed an offence in keeping this child here for so long? Why didn't you immediately phone the police, when you found her on the twenty-first of December?'

So Amber told her the whole story. Eventually the policewoman said, 'We shall, of course, be taking Pearl straight back to her foster mother, but I have to warn you, Miss Jacobs, that you will be obliged to accompany us to a police station to help us with our enquiries...'

With a start, Pearl realised what this meant, and threw her arms round Amber.

'Amber hasn't done anything wrong!' she shouted. 'It's all *my* fault, if you want to know! I begged and begged her to help me find Mum, and then I begged and begged her to let me stay for Christmas. You *can't* arrest her! She's the best friend I ever had, and she's looked after me, and cooked me lovely meals, and cheered me up when I felt sad. And just *look* at all my nice clothes and presents!' Pearl flushed dark with anger.

The policewoman smiled at Pearl. 'I understand what you are saying, Pearl, but we do have to take Miss Jacobs in for questioning. Now, you be a good girl, and say goodbye to her. We have a police car waiting outside for you, and you'll soon be back safe and sound with your foster mum.'

While Amber packed all her clothes and presents in a big hold-all, Pearl found Tiggy hiding in her box, and gave her a hug and a kiss.

She threw her arms round Amber. 'You will remember what you promised, won't you?' she choked.

'I promise, Pearl, I promise,' said Amber.

Tears poured down Pearl's face as the policewoman gently uncurled her from Amber's arms, and led her along the tow path to the waiting police car. From the back seat she saw Amber, tall, upright and unsmiling, being taken to another car.

Chapter 17

Pearl woke up with a start. Something was wrong. Where was Tiggy? Why was the boat so still? And why did everything *smell* strange?

She sat up with a start.

Of course! She wasn't on the boat – she was back in her old bedroom in Jenny's house.

She ached with loss – for Amber, for Tiggy, for the boat. Then she felt the crackle of an envelope underneath her pillow, and pressed it close to her cheek. A comforting warmth flowed through her.

It was her second day back at Jenny's. How strange it had all been – what a crazy mix of feelings had swirled around inside her in that short time, as she see-sawed from despair and bewilderment, to hope.

The first surprise was that Jenny wasn't angry with her. When the police car drew up outside the house, Jenny had dashed down the garden path to meet Pearl, her face lit up with happiness.

And she had hugged her, and called her a silly sausage, and cried, and told her how glad she was to have her back safe and sound. Later, when the police had gone, Jenny had sat down on the sofa next to Pearl.

'What I don't understand, chick, is why you felt you had to run away?'

So Pearl had told her everything. About how she was terrified Jenny would say she was a thief, and not want to look after her any more – and that she would be sent to a Home.

'And when I heard Mum was missing, I was so *sure*, Jenny, that she would go back to the boat, and wait for me there, but…'

Jenny had patted her hand gently, and passed her a paper tissue. She had given Pearl a cuddle, and said she understood, and *of course* she still wanted Pearl to live with her. 'And there's *no way* anyone's going to send you to a Home, chicken, – you can stay here as long as you need to!'

She had taken Pearl into the front room, and there was a Christmas tree, still standing in its little red pot, all a-twinkle with lights and rainbow baubles.

And underneath the Christmas tree was a big stack of presents.

Pearl had turned in bewilderment towards Jenny. 'Who are they for?'

'For you, Pearl, for you, chick – from lots of people. We all hoped and prayed you would come back in time for Christmas. I've kept the fairy lights on all the time, so you would see them through the window, if you came back—'

Pearl felt a hot pricking in her nose, and flung her arms round Jenny. 'Oh Jenny, I didn't know so many people really cared about me!'

She had sat down by the tree, and opened her presents one by one. There was a gorgeous long frilled skirt, in peach, from Jenny, and a cream top to go with it. There were sweets, and chocolates, and a book of ghost stories with a really spooky cover. There was a kit for making friendship bracelets from Bernie, a camera from Kathy and Jamal, and a huge bundle of letters and cards from everyone in her class at school.

Pearl was stunned. 'So they don't all hate me?' she had whispered.

'No, Pearl, of course they don't,' smiled Jenny. 'And Grace has been round every single day to ask about you, and she gave me this for you.'

Wonderingly Pearl had unwrapped the shiny gold paper. Inside was a tiny silver ring with a dolphin on it, and a matching silver bracelet.

'She must still like me,' Pearl's voice quivered.

'Of course she does, chick; look, I think everyone understands why you took those books. They know you're not a bad girl really.'

It had all been too much; but there was more to come.

'I've been saving this for you, Pearl.' Jenny gave Pearl an envelope.

It said:

For Pearl

And it was in her mum's handwriting.

Quickly Pearl had torn it open.

Inside was a beautiful Christmas card, with a Father Christmas in the snow. When you opened it, it played *Jingle bells*. And underneath, in spidery handwriting, Pearl read:

> *To Pearl, my treasure,*
> *with all my love,*
> *Mummy*

There was a little note at the bottom of the card. It said:

> *I'm sorry I can't be with you this Christmas, but I HAVEN'T FORGOTTEN YOU, Pearl, and I never, ever will. Only I've been feeling a bit muddled, and as soon as I get my head straight, I'll write a proper letter.*
>
> *Love you lots and lots,*
> *Mummy XXXXXXXXXXXXXXXXXXX*

Pearl held the letter closely to her chest, her heart beating wildly.

Mum hadn't forgotten about her!

She was out there, somewhere – *and she still loved her*.

She turned to Jenny, her eyes shining brightly. To her astonishment, Pearl saw tears glistening in Jenny's eyes.

'I know, I know, Pearl,' she said. 'And the police are busy right now, looking for her.'

'One day,' said Pearl, and her voice was strong, 'one day soon, we'll be together again.'

And through all that followed, Pearl kept this hope alive and well in her heart.

Later in the day there had been a great commotion in the street at the front of the house. Pearl had run to the window. Instantly, the world exploded in a series of violent flashes.

She jumped back, startled.

Jenny rushed to the front door.

'You can all go *away*!' she shouted. 'She's a little *child*, for heaven's sake! Now, either you clear off this minute, or I'll call the police!'

And Jenny did just that. Within minutes a police car had arrived, and the whole street was empty.

'What did they want?' Pearl was shocked.

'You, chick, you!' She sat Pearl down gently onto a chair. 'Pearl, all of England knows you've been missing, and everyone is very, very glad you've been found. But there's no way I'm going to let that bunch of vultures anywhere near you!'

After tea Jenny let Pearl watch a bit of the news.

There on the screen her own face grinned back at her!

She blushed, and hid her face in her hands.

'The missing schoolgirl, Pearl Lovett, has been found alive and well,' said the announcer, smiling broadly. 'Pearl is believed to have been staying on a canal boat previously owned by her mother. A woman is helping the police with their enquiries.'

Pearl turned, horrified, to Jenny. 'Did people really think I might be dead?' She saw Jenny's face, and her heart gave a lurch. 'I'm sorry, Jenny,' she whispered, 'I'm so sorry.'

But Jenny had just held her tight, and said, 'There, there, chick, there, there.'

Pearl had been very subdued for the rest of the evening. For the first time she began to realise what she had done. And she worried and worried about Amber.

As she had sat curled up in a corner of the sofa she had heard the phone ring. Jenny had came into the room smiling broadly. 'Grace wants to talk to you, Pearl. She's so excited!'

But Pearl had shaken her head. 'I don't want to talk to her just yet, Jenny. Can you say I'm sorry – and I'll – I'll phone tomorrow?'

Part of her longed to see Grace again, but there was

still that nasty, squirmy feeling in her tummy – that Grace might not really, really like her anymore…

The next day Bernie came round. Pearl had been worried about meeting Bernie – would she be angry with her, after all she'd done for Pearl?

But Bernie's face was wreathed in smiles as she leaped up the garden path and she gave Pearl a warm hug.

'Thank you for my Christmas present,' said Pearl shyly.

Jenny bustled in with tea and cakes, and everyone got very merry. After tea Jenny left Bernie alone with Pearl, and Bernie asked her so many questions about how Amber had treated her, that Pearl felt her head was going to burst.

'I keep telling everyone, Bernie,' she said crossly. 'Amber never hurt a hair on my head. She's the kindest person in the world!'

'OK, Pearl,' said Bernie. 'But there's just one thing I don't understand, love. When you got to Broughton, and your mum wasn't there, why did you stay on the boat so long? Did Amber try to make you?'

'NO!' shouted Pearl. 'It was all my fault! I keep telling everyone – I didn't want to leave the boat, because it's my *home* – and Tiggy's there as well – and Amber, she was really kind to me, and…and, she *understands* me, because she lost her mum, just like me. And now she's gone and got into trouble because of me!'

Then Bernie smiled, and said, 'OK, Pearl, you win!' and wrote something down in her notebook.

'You will tell the police it's all my fault, won't you, Bernie?' said Pearl anxiously. 'Or Amber might be in big, big trouble.'

'Of course I will, Pearl. And another thing – we have good hopes of finding your mum, now she's contacted Social Services with your letter. So try not to worry so much about everything, love. Let the grown ups sort it out!'

Chapter 18

It was all very well leaving everything to the grown ups, thought Pearl. She tried to put her worries of her mind, but as the days went by with no news of either her mum or Amber, she couldn't help worrying.

Was Amber OK?

Was she back on the boat?

And who was looking after Tiggy?

And then there was the big question: *Where was Mum?*

On the Friday before school began again, the phone rang early in the morning. Pearl pricked up her ears.

'Oh hello, Mrs Joseph! Yes, she's fine...I tell you what, I'll have a word with her now... Can you hold on a minute?'

Jenny turned to Pearl.

'I've got Grace's mum on the phone, chick — Grace is dying to see you! Why don't we invite her for tea?

After all, you'll be going back to school next week – and I think it'll be a lot easier if you've at least seen Grace first…'

Pearl's head was in a whirl. She felt really guilty – she knew she should have phoned Grace to thank her for her Christmas present, but she just couldn't face it. And of course, on Monday, school started…and she would have to face everyone again…

Suddenly she made up her mind. 'OK, Jenny. Let Grace come for tea.'

All day long Pearl fretted. It was so embarrassing! Whatever would she say to Grace; and would Grace still really, *really* like her?

At four thirty promptly, the door bell rang. Jenny leaped to her feet. Pearl froze. She was in the middle of icing some cherry buns for tea. Icing dripped all over the kitchen floor. She strained her ears.

Voices in the hall.

Suddenly, a smiling face peeped round the kitchen door.

Pearl felt her face burning. 'Hi,' she whispered.

Grace came right up to her, and threw her arms round her. Icing flew all round the kitchen. A big blob landed on Grace's nose.

'Oh Grace!' gasped Pearl. 'Oh Grace!'

There was a split second of silence, and then they both burst into howls of laughter.

'Well, I see you've broken the ice,' laughed Jenny looking round the door.

'No, we've broken the ICING!' said Grace, and they collapsed again into helpless giggles.

'Oh, get on with you!' said Jenny. 'Go on upstairs and amuse yourselves Pearl's room for a bit, while I sort out this lot!'

Pearl and Grace ran upstairs, breathless with laughter.

They sat down on Pearl's bed, and talked and talked.

Somehow the silliness and the laughter released something deep inside Pearl. She found herself pouring out the whole story – everything that had happened since the day she had run away.

Grace listened spellbound. Her eyes grew enormous as Pearl told her about the night in the woods, and the old hollow oak tree. 'You're so brave, Pearl – I would've been really scared!'

'I was,' admitted Pearl. 'But I kept on thinking about…about seeing Mum, and that sort of helped…only when I got to the boat, she wasn't there. And then I met Amber, and she was so good to me. And then Tiggy turned up! I really didn't want to leave everything, and come back, 'cause I thought everyone would be really angry with me, and they'd put me in a Home…'

Grace nodded, and took Pearl's hand to show she understood.

'And now something very, very special has happened,

Grace. I've had a really beautiful Christmas card from my mum – Social Services sent it on – and she said she hadn't forgotten about me, and she loves me lots and lots…it's just that she's been so ill, you see—'

Grace clapped her hands to her mouth. 'Oh Pearl, that's really, really great!'

'And Bernie says the police have good hopes of finding her soon…' Pearl looked at Grace with shining eyes. 'The only thing is, you know my friend Amber, right? Well, she's in trouble because of me – and I don't know if she's all right, and who's looking after Tiggy. And I've caused so much *trouble*, Grace – I'm sorry, really sorry I left you like that—'

'Give over, you wally,' said Grace, 'It don't matter a bit. You're back home, right – that's what matters.'

And she gave Pearl a big hug.

They had a fantastic evening. Jenny had cooked home-made pizza with salad for tea. And then they had trifle and the cherry buns – a bit splodgy in places, but they tasted really good.

After tea they went back up to Pearl's room, and played at being pop-stars. Grace was Chanterelle, and Pearl was Shayenne. Then Grace showed Pearl some of the things she'd learned in ballet lessons, and they both twirled around in old net curtains, doing Swan Lake.

The time sped by, and both girls were amazed when

Grace's mum appeared to take her home.

'Oh, does she *have* to go now?' said Pearl. 'Can't she stay a little bit longer?'

But Mrs Josephs said Grace had to be in bed early, because she had a ballet lesson first thing in the morning. 'But I tell you what – how about if Grace comes round after breakfast on Monday morning, so you can go to school together?'

Pearl nodded gratefully. She'd been dreading that first morning. It would be so much easier with Grace standing by her.

On Saturday morning a letter shot through the letter box addressed to Pearl. It had a Leicestershire postmark.

Amber! It must be from Amber!

Pearl tore open the envelope.

Dear Pearl,

Hi, sweetheart, how are you? I'm sorry I haven't written before, but I had to sort everything out with the police and social services – but everything's OK now. The police kept me all day at the station, and asked me so many questions you wouldn't believe it. Anyway, in the end they decided to let me go back to the boat so I could look after Tiggy and everything.

I had to promise to report to the police station first thing in the morning, so of course I did, and then there were MORE questions, till my head was spinning! In the end they decided not to charge me with any offence. I think what you told your social worker helped.

And I'm allowed to write to you, but not to see you - not at the moment, anyway - but I've written to Social Services, and your Bernie is going to come and see me next week.

SO KEEP YOUR ~~FINGERS~~ CROSSED!

Tigs is very well, and as naughty as usual, but I think she misses you. I do too, Pearl, and I'm going to do everything I can to keep in touch with you. I'll go on at Bernie till she's so fed-up she lets me visit you!

I hope everything works out well at your foster mum's, Pearl. I think Jenny must be a very special person, you know. I know you'd rather be with your mum, and I'm sure that she'll be found soon. I'd love to hear from you sweetheart—

with lots of love,
your friend Amber

xxxxxxxxxxxxxxxx

Tucked in with the letter was a beautiful drawing of Tiggy, curled up in her box, signed, *With purrs and cuddles, from Tiggy.*

There were three pawprints underneath.

Pearl felt a great weight drop off her.

Amber was OK.

She hadn't been sent to prison – and she might be allowed to visit! Pearl gave the picture of Tiggy a resounding kiss. Then she turned to Jenny.

'Do you want to read it, Jen?'

'If you don't mind?'

Jenny read the letter in silence.

'She sounds a really nice person, your friend Amber…and she can draw, can't she!'

'Oh yes, she's brill,' said Pearl. She ran and fetched her poetry anthology to show Jenny.

'Would you like her to visit you, Pearl?'

'More than anything in the world – apart from finding Mum, that is,' said Pearl seriously.

'Well, we'll see,' said Jenny. 'I'll talk to Bernie about it.'

All too soon the weekend was over. On Sunday evening Pearl crept into bed with a heavy heart. However was she going to face Monday?

Next morning her heart beat fast as she got dressed for school. She was trying to force down some toast to please Jenny, when the door bell rang. Thank goodness for Grace!

They set off really early. Pearl's footsteps began to drag as they neared the school. When they reached the main gates, she just couldn't bring herself to go in. Whatever would Mrs Parsons say to her? And just suppose she met Mrs Jackson in the corridor!

'Come on, Pearl,' said Grace encouragingly. 'There's no one around. Anyway, everyone'll be *glad* to see you!'

Then suddenly Mrs Parsons was there. She ran beaming towards both girls.

'Pearl, how lovely to have you back! Grace, you're a star!' She put an arm round each girl, and swept them across the playground, up the steps, and through the main doors.

In the classroom Tom was sorting out the art cupboard.

'Hi, Pearl,' he grinned, and as if nothing had happened since he last saw her, he went back to stacking paint trays.

'Go and give Tom a hand, plese girls, will you?' said Mrs Parsons. 'He's struggling on his own. If someone could wash those trays out, it would be wonderful!'

Pearl was so busy at the sink, watching the dried paint dissolve and swirl down the drain in multicoloured patterns, that she hardly noticed the other children drifting into the classroom. She finished just in time to sit down next to Grace for registration.

Pearl couldn't believe it – everyone was so friendly!

OK – not quite everyone; Amy didn't speak to her, or even look at her, but she didn't say one mean word, and with Grace clucking round Pearl like a mother hen, she began to relax.

And to her astonishment, she really enjoyed the day.

They had maths first thing. Pearl struggled a bit, but Mrs Parsons came and sat by her and helped her, so that was all right. Afterwards they could choose a book and read on their own. She escaped blissfully into a book, and then after break it was art. They were allowed to paint anything they liked. Pearl did a picture of herself and Amber round the Christmas tree, with Tiggy fighting the wrapping paper.

'Oh Pearl, I wish I could paint like that,' said Grace.

'Definitely one for the wall,' said Mrs Parsons.

Pearl blushed. 'One day, I'd like to be real artist, like Amber,' she whispered to Grace.

After dinner it was dance in the big hall. Pearl whirled around to the music, her heart light for the first time in ages. Everything was just the same: Jamie Kershaw had to sit on the side and watch, for being silly as usual; Amy showed off all over the place, but no one took any notice; and Grace got a merit for beautiful dancing.

And *still* no one said a word to her about what had happened.

*

Grace walked all the way back home with her.

'You know, Grace, I really like Willowbrook,' said Pearl thoughtfully. 'It's the nicest school I've ever been to.'

'Me too,' said Grace. 'Sort of friendly.'

As Pearl turned the corner of her road, she saw a little red car parked outside her house. She skipped up the garden path, and ran into the living room.

There was Bernie, sitting on the sofa. Her face was wreathed in smiles.

'We've found your mum, Pearl,' she said.

Chapter 19

'Can we go a bit faster Bernie, *please*?' Pearl pushed her feet hard against the front seat, willing the car on.

'Pearl!' Bernie laughed. 'We're doing nearly seventy miles an hour as it is – and that's the speed limit, young lady! We'll be there soon enough!'

Pearl sighed. Everything had been so *slow* since that marvellous afternoon when Bernie told her that her mum had been found in Manchester. She'd thought that Bernie would take her up there straightaway – or at least first thing in the morning.

How wrong she had been!

First they had to wait while her mum spent a week in a hospital in Manchester recovering.

'She's been really poorly, you see, chick,' Jenny had explained. 'She hasn't been eating properly for weeks, and she's been sleeping out in the cold. She needs care, and nursing to get her on her feet again.'

Then it was decided that Mum should be transferred back to Beechwood Hospital in Birmingham. Bernie said Mum had agreed to go as a voluntary patient, and that was good.

Another long week passed, until at last the hospital phoned Bernie, and said Mum was well enough for Pearl to visit. And now it was Saturday morning, and Pearl was on her way up the M1 to Birmingham.

'I'm going to pull in at the next service station, Pearl. Time for a loo stop...and how about a drink and a jam doughnut?'

Pearl sighed. If only Bernie would just put her foot down and get on!

As soon as they walked in the motorway service station, Pearl noticed the shop. Presents! She could get something for Mum.

'I thought you'd got some presents for Mum in your bag,' said Bernie. 'Jenny told me you'd made her a wonderful necklace.'

Pearl nodded. 'And I've made her a tinful of chocolate brownies – she really loves those, you know – and I've done a painting for her as well. But I want to get her something *really special* from the shop. I've saved up lots of pocket money – look!' Pearl waved a five pound note at Bernie.

'OK, Pearl – if that's what you want!'

Pearl walked slowly round the shop, staring at all the gifts. What should she buy? A cuddly toy? A fluffy bunny with sad eyes just begged to be picked up and cuddled. He would make Mum laugh.

Or what about a beautiful make-up bag?

Or a big box of Belgian chocolates?

Then Pearl saw it: a little glass jewellery box, with a stained glass rainbow on the lid. All round the sides were flying birds, a kingfisher, a robin, a swallow…

In a dream Pearl picked up the box, and drifted over to the check out. The assistant tucked it up carefully in bubble wrap. She smiled at Pearl. 'Present, is it?'

Pearl nodded.

'Tell you what – I'll do it up special for you!' She wrapped it in deep blue tissue paper, and tied it with curly silver ribbon. 'There you go, dear!'

'Oh, thank you!' Pearl smiled shyly at the lady, and turned to Bernie. 'It's perfect now, really perfect!'

Pearl clutched the present to her while she munched her way through a very satisfactory jammy doughnut.

'I thought you weren't hungry!' laughed Bernie.

Pearl didn't answer. She was eighty miles away, in Birmingham, seeing the moment when she gave the jewellery box to Mum…

Back on the motorway, they soon started to see signs to the M6, and Birmingham. Pearl's spirits started to soar.

'Only forty miles now, Bernie!' she shouted. And she started to sing.

157

Bernie was brilliant. They sang their way all through *One Man Went to Mow* and *Ten Green Bottles*. Then Pearl did her Shayenne impressions for Bernie, and had her in stitches.

Soon they were on the M6. Beechwood was the other side of Birmingham, so Bernie said they would have to go round Spaghetti Junction.

'Spaghetti Junction!' Pearl burst out. 'Whatever's that?'

'It's where the motorways all join, and they twist and turn every which way, like spaghetti,' explained Bernie. 'You'll soon see.'

Pearl loved Spaghetti Junction. It was a bit like being on a roller coaster at the fair – not as fast, of course, but wonderfully twisty and turny. It made Pearl deliciously dizzy.

And then, suddenly, there was a roundabout and they were off the motorway.

How slowly there were travelling now! Pearl found her feet pushing hard again at the front seat.

'It won't make us go any faster, love, honestly it won't,' said Bernie.

And then they hit a traffic jam.

'It's no use fretting, Pearl,' said Bernie. 'We'll just have to sit it out.' She passed her a mint.

They sat and they sat, edging forwards a little bit at a time. The car got hot and stuffy, but when Bernie opened the window, horrible fumes came in, and she had to shut it straightaway. Pearl sighed. It was so annoying, when they were so near…

'Bernie, if Mum's really lots better, do you think they will let her out soon?'

'I don't know, love.' Bernie sounded serious. 'The letter I had from the hospital said your mum was making good progress. But you have to remember, Pearl, she'd been sleeping rough for several weeks before the police found her – and she hadn't been eating properly, either. And with her other illness – you know, the sickness in her mind – we just don't know yet how stable she is, and whether the medicine has had time to work—'

'But she's taking her medicine now, and the nurses are looking after her, and everything,' faltered Pearl. 'She *will* get better, won't she?'

'I really hope so, Pearl, but we musn't expect too much too soon, you know…'

For a moment the day darkened, then Pearl gave an annoyed sniff. Bernie was just being a bit of an old misery guts, the way grown ups sometimes were.

And now the traffic seemed to be speeding up.

'Here we go again!' said Bernie. 'Should be there in about fifteen minutes, at this rate!'

Pearl's heart did a flip-flop. Fifteen minutes, and she would be with Mum!

In fact they reached the hospital in less than ten minutes. Pearl saw a big sign, saying *BEECHWOOD*

HOSPITAL and an arrow pointing down a long tree-lined drive. In the borders snowdrops were already out, and here and there crocuses glowed purple and gold.

Pearl was really surprised – she had imagined a nasty, tall building, all dark and gloomy with old-fashioned towers. But Beechwood hospital was built from creamy gold bricks that gleamed softly in the sunlight. The windows were wide, and hung with cheerful curtains, and in front of the house a flower bed was set out with evergreen shrubs. Tiny daffodils nodded in the wind, and baskets filled with winter pansies and primulas hung outside the front door.

Pearl tiptoed behind Bernie across the polished wooden floor of the reception area.

'We've come to see Melissa Lovett,' said Bernie to the receptionist.

Pearl tapped her feet impatiently, while the lady scanned her computer.

'Ward twenty-five,' she smiled. 'Take the lift to level two, and turn right.'

In the lift Pearl began to shiver. Bernie clasped her hand warmly.

'It's all going to be fine, love,' she whispered. 'Just fine.'

A minute later they were walking along a pink painted corridor, hung with beautiful paintings. Ahead of them double doors said:

Ward 23
Please ring the bell, and wait.

Bernie rang.

A smiling young lady opened the door. She was wearing a badge that said *Karen*.

'We're here to see Melissa Lovett.' said Bernie.

'I thought you probably were,' said Karen. She smiled at Pearl. 'You must be Pearl! Your mum's so excited about seeing you!'

A long walk down another corridor, and then Karen paused outside a room which said *Visitors' Room*.

A small nurse with thick, dark curls showed them in. She beamed at Pearl and Bernie. *Her* badge said *Marie*.

'She's here, Melissa!' she called.

A tall, haggard lady got up slowly from a chair. Pearl's heart skipped a beat. She was the thinnest person Pearl had ever seen. Her face seemed strangely yellow, and her eyes had huge dark shadows. Her hair was dull and lanky, and there were bruises on her arms. Surely she was not…surely not?

But she was walking towards Pearl, with her arms outstretched.

Pearl looked closely at that thin, haggard face.

She looked into the eyes and she knew.

It was Mum.

Pearl took a wobbly step forward, and then she was in

her mother's arms. Underneath the horrible antiseptic hospital smell the warm comforting scent of bread and roses was still there, faint but unmistakable.

For several long moments they clung together, and when Pearl looked up, she saw that her mother's face was streaming with tears.

'Oh Pearly, my Pearly,' whispered Mum. 'Let me look at you!'

She held Pearl at arms length.

'You've grown so much!' she said, her voice all blurry with tears.

Pearl gazed back silently at her mother, numb with shock. After all this long wait, after all this time, and all the longing, she could find nothing to say.

Whatever had happened to her mum? Where were her plump, rosy cheeks? What had happened to her shiny copper hair? And why was she so *thin*?

Her mother took her by the hand, and led her to a sofa. Pearl sat down next to her, still unable to talk. She felt her mother's hand gently stroking her hair, and began to tremble.

At last words came. 'Oh Mum, oh Mum,' she whispered. 'I've wanted you so much!'

'Me too, baby,' said her mum. Gently she wiped away the tears from Pearl's eyes.

'I've bought you some presents,' sniffed Pearl. She fished in her bag. 'I made this 'specially for you.'

Pearl handed her mother a little packet wrapped in gold paper.

Inside was the peacock necklace.

'Oh Pearl – *peacocks*!' Mum's face lit up. 'You remembered!'

She slipped the necklace on. Pearl helped her with the fastening.

'It's the most beautiful necklace I have ever had, Pearl.' Her eyes were full of tears. She turned to Marie. 'There – I told you – Pearl's artistic, just like me!'

Everyone smiled, and then Pearl brought out the chocolate brownies.

'Wow, look at those!' said Marie. 'Shall I get some plates and drinks? We'll have ourselves a little party!'

She whisked out of the room, and returned a few minutes later with a pot of tea, four blue mugs, and some plates.

Pearl noticed that Mum hadn't spoken a single word to Bernie. Didn't she like her? But there was no time to worry about that, because Marie had set out the brownies on a pretty china plate, and Mum was busy pouring tea into the mugs.

'These are great, Pearl,' said Bernie, munching away.

'Oh, my Pearl's always been a good cook,' said Mum quickly, turning to Bernie. 'I taught her, you know.'

'You certainly taught her well,' said Marie. 'These are delicious.'

'Jenny helped me,' said Pearl shyly.

She felt her mother stiffen beside her on the sofa.

'Only she's not as good a cook as you are, Mum.' she added hastily.

'Now I've got something for *you*, Pearly,' said her mum. 'I'm really sorry I couldn't get you a present for Christmas, darling…but I made this for you myself.'

She pulled something pink and crinkly out of her bag. It was tied with curly lilac ribbons. On the front, was a silver gift tag. It said:

To Pearl, my treasure,
with all my love,
Mummy.

Pearl opened the present with shaky fingers, trying not to tear the pretty paper.

Inside, wrapped in white tissue paper, was a little lilac cardigan. It had pearly buttons, and embroidered on the front was a tiny rainbow.

It was much too small for her.

'Oh Mum, it's lovely,' Pearl longed to put it on but there was no way it would fit. She draped it round her shoulders.

'It's gorgeous, isn't it?' said Marie. 'I just wish I could knit like that! You know, Pearl, your mum's been working away at that night and day to get it finished in time.'

Pearl looked up at her mother. 'It's the most beautiful cardigan in the world!' she said. 'And...and I've got something else for you, too!'

Pearl lifted the dark blue parcel out of her bag, and gave it to her mum. Anxiously she waited while Mum undid the silver ribbon.

'Oh Pearl – a *rainbow*! It's got a rainbow on the lid!'

She put the little jewellery box down on the table, and hugged Pearl fiercely.

'You see – rainbows are special to us,' she said to Bernie and Marie. 'We're rainbow people, you know!'

Her eyes lit up, and she leaped out of her chair. 'Come on, Pearl – come and see my bedroom!'

'Perhaps we should all go together—' began Marie.

She was too late. Pearl's mum had grabbed her by the hand and was pulling her along a corridor. They stopped outside a little room.

'Ta-raaa!' she cried, throwing open the door.

Pearl stepped nervously into the room, and stopped dead.

Every single wall, every tiny space, was covered with rainbows: paintings of rainbows; hand-made rainbow mobiles; rainbow crystals; and arching across the window, a huge rainbow made from special tissue paper that let the light shine through.

Rainbow light flashed around the room.

'Oh Mum – it's beautiful!' whispered Pearl.

Then she noticed something. On the little cabinet beside the bed there was a photograph of her – the same as the one she had in her Life Story book back at Jenny's. It was the one of her when she was about two, in the little red leggings, and the rainbow-embroidered top.

'I didn't know you had that photo too, Mum!' she cried.

'I've carried it everywhere with me, Pearly, everywhere – in the back of my purse. You've always been with me, my treasure.'

Pearl felt tears welling up in her throat.

'We will be together again, soon, Mum, won't we?'

'Soon as I get out of here, as soon as this mucking lot let me go!'

Suddenly her mood changed.

Her face twisted with anger and her eyes went hard and wrong. For a moment Pearl felt afraid. Then outside the room she heard footsteps. Marie's smiling face peeped round the door.

'Hi – everything all right?'

'It was until you stuck your nose in,' snapped Pearl's mother. 'We're fine, Pearly and me, we don't need any busybodies, thank you.'

'Why don't we all go back to the visitor's room, Melissa – the tea's going cold.' Marie put her arm gently around Mum's shoulders.

But her mother shook Marie off and pulled Pearl fiercely towards her. 'Come on, baby – we're the rainbow people – remember?'

She threw back her head, and started to laugh.

Clasping Pearl tightly, Mum began to dance. Her face went smiley again, and Pearl relaxed. Down the corridor they twirled. Her mum was singing 'Somewhere, over the rainbow' very loudly.

'Come on, everyone, let's celebrate. It's a rainbow day – and I've got my beautiful, rainbow daughter back!'

Pearl clung breathlessly to her mother, as the world whirled by. The pictures on the wall cartwheeled past. Faces swirled in and out of focus.

'Let's show them, Pearly, come on girlie – it's whirly-twirly time!' said Mum. Laughing and singing she spun them down the corridor and into the visitor's room.

At first Pearl laughed too, but Mum went on whirling and twirling faster and faster, and now she was laughing much too loudly, in a silly, high voice.

Pearl began to feel sick. 'Let's stop now, Mum,' she gasped, 'I'm getting dizzy!'

But Mum didn't stop.

Faster and faster she twirled, as if she was never going to stop, crying, 'Whirly-twirly, who's my Pearly?'

And then Pearl knew.

Her mum had flipped.

In the distance she heard voices.

'Come on now, Melissa,' said a gentle, reasonable voice. 'Pearl's had enough now. Come and sit down for a bit.'

167

But Mum didn't stop. She was whirling Pearl round so fast that Pearl had to close her eyes. Any minute now, she would be sick. She couldn't hold it down any longer.

A bell started ringing loudly, and suddenly there were other voices in the room. Pearl felt her mother being pulled away from her. She staggered, as chairs and tables spun past her. Then strong arms caught her and set her down gently on the sofa.

She was shaking all over. Slowly the dizziness and the nausea left her.

In the distance her mother was shouting, 'Let me go! I want my daughter! Why are you all taking me away from my daughter!'

Suddenly there was the unmistakable sound of smashing china.

Something flew across the room, and caught Pearl sharply on the arm.

It was the rainbow box.

Frozen with terror, Pearl felt someone scoop her up and carry her out of the room.

Chapter 20

Pearl was running along a dark corridor. She knew she had to run like mad, because she was being chased by a skeleton. Her heart pounded in her ears as she tried to run faster, but her legs wouldn't work, and bit by bit the skeleton was gaining on her.

Frantically she looked behind her. The skeleton was only a few metres away now, and as she looked, it grew flesh and changed into her mum.

'Stop, Pearl, stop! Come and dance with me, baby!' shouted the Skeleton Mum.

Gasping Pearl tried to force herself forward, but now her legs had turned to water, and she couldn't move.

'Stop, stop! It's only me, Pearly,' cried the Skeleton Mum. And she scooped Pearl into her arms and started to whirl her round in a fast, jerky dance.

Suddenly the Skeleton Mum smiled. As Pearl looked at her, she changed into her real, smiley mum, the mum with the rosy cheeks and the copper hair.

Pearl sighed with relief, and smiled back, but the face changed again and this time it was angry and twisted.

'Why are you running away from me?' said the Skeleton Mum. 'Why, why?'

And she began to dance faster and faster, until Pearl knew she was going to be sick.

Then the world exploded, and broken glass showered all around her.

Pearl screamed, and sat bolt upright in bed. Her heart was pounding, and she was shaking and drenched with sweat.

Jenny came running into the room. 'All right, chicken, it's all right, I've got you.' She put her arms round Pearl and held her tight until the shuddering stopped. 'Was it a nightmare, love?'

Pearl nodded.

'Do you want to tell me about it?'

Pearl hesitated. Somehow she couldn't tell anyone, even Jenny, about the full awfulness of that dream…

'I dreamed about Mum…and she wasn't my mum, but something else…something nasty…and she was chasing me…and I couldn't get away—' Pearl shivered violently.

Her arm was hurting where the glass rainbow box had caught her yesterday. She felt it tenderly.

After Bernie had carried her to safety, out of all that terror, a nurse had cleaned the cut on her arm. It was too

170

deep for a plaster, so Pearl had had to go with Bernie to the Accident and Emergency department of the hospital, and have the cut stitched.

It had hurt, but she had tried hard not to make a fuss. Everyone said she was very brave.

Then Bernie had taken her for a hot drink, and cuddled her and comforted her until she was well enough to be taken back to Jenny's.

'Is your arm hurting, chick?' Jenny's gentle voice broke into her dreams.

Pearl nodded.

'Come on downstairs with me, and I'll give you some Calpol, and a warm drink.' Jenny slipped Pearl's dressing gown carefully round her shoulders and led her downstairs.

Later, exhausted but comforted, Pearl fell asleep.

In the morning, first thing, Bernie came round.

Jenny had a few moments in private with Bernie. Then she made her a coffee, and left her alone with Pearl.

'How are you feeling, love?' Bernie patted Pearl's hand gently.

'Better…I don't know—' Pearl's voice trailed off.

How *did* she feel?

And how could she ever really tell anyone that she thought her mother was a *monster*? That she was *mad*?

'I guess you must be feeling pretty muddled, Pearl?'

171

Pearl looked up. How did Bernie always *know*?

She sat in silence for a moment, re-living all that had happened yesterday.

She remembered how excited she had been, how wonderful it had been to see her mother again, how Mum had held her close. How she had smelled that warm, comforting smell, the smell of bread and roses, that meant Mum, and love, and security…

And then she forced her mind to remember the things she didn't want to see.

That ugly, angry look on her mother's face before she flipped…

Those awful minutes when her mum wouldn't stop dancing and whirled her round and round, till she was terrified and sick…

The shouting, the exploding glass, the pain in her arm…

'Bernie, can I ask you a question?' Pearl's voice wavered.

'Of course you can, love. You can ask me anything.'

'Is my mum…? Is my mum…is she *mad*?'

Bernie sighed. 'Mad's a tricky word, Pearl. Sometimes it's hard to say who's mad, and who's sane. Sometimes we can all be a bit mad! We all have mood swings – you know, good days, and bad days, but your mum's mood swings are much more violent than that. It's an illness of the mind. She gets very low, sometimes, and then very high. A lot of the time, she's as reasonable as you or me, but sometimes, everything gets out of control, and—'

'She flips,' said Pearl bitterly.

'Yes, Pearl – she flips. The thing is, if she takes her medicine all the time, we know that she will be much less likely to have these terrible mood swings…but you see, when she was on her own up in Manchester, she didn't take it for a long time. Then after a few weeks back on her medication at Beechwood, the staff thought that she was much better, and it would be OK for you to visit…but I guess it was too soon—'

'Will she ever really get better?'

'We can't say for sure, Pearl, but she'll probably need to be on medication for the rest of her life, and if she doesn't take it… And then there's her drinking problem, too.'

Pearl nodded silently. Everything was suddenly very clear to her.

Very cold, and very clear.

'And that's why, Pearl, we've been trying to find you a Forever Family. Someone to love and care for you while you're growing up. To keep you safe… Of course, that doesn't mean you can't see your mum sometimes, and write to her whenever you want, and always keep in touch with her. We know how much she loves you, and how much you love her…'

Pearl's feelings buzzed dizzily in her head.

Did she still love her mum? She thought of the mad Skeleton Mum in the dream and shuddered. Slowly she raised her head, and looked Bernie straight in the eyes.

'Sometimes… Sometimes, I feel as if I hate her. And she really scares me.'

There – she'd said it.

'Of course you do, love – after all you've been through, that's only natural. But that's not the whole story, is it?

Pearl shook her head. 'I hate her – and I love her too,' she whispered. Sudden tears filled her eyes, and she buried her head in her hands, and sobbed.

Bernie let her cry. She held Pearl's hand and let her cry until she had cried herself dry. Then she handed Pearl a paper tissue for her nose.

'You know, there's one thing you must understand, Pearl…it's not your mum's fault she's like this. It's a terrible illness – and she's no more responsible for it than you would be if you got the chicken pox.'

This was a new way of looking at things. For the first time Pearl started to understand how dreadful the illness must be for her mother.

And she knew something else, too.

She couldn't live with Mum anymore.

She loved her – oh, so much. Into her mind came the picture of her mum's bedroom at the hospital, filled with rainbows, and the little photo of herself which Mum had carried everywhere with her. Everywhere – in hospital; on the streets of Manchester. A lump came into Pearl's throat, and she caught her breath.

But she knew now that she could never make Mum

better, and she knew she couldn't live with her.

She looked at Bernie. 'You know that Forever Family?'

Bernie nodded.

'Well, I don't want to live with Kathy and Jamal; they're ever so nice, it's not that – but I know what I want, now.'

She looked earnestly at Bernie.

'I want to live with Amber.'

Chapter 21

'And I want to cook a proper *boat* tea for her – you know, bacon and eggs and things.'

Pearl danced joyfully alongside Jenny. Every now and then she did a little dance.

'That's fine by me, chicken. Careful, you'll have that old lady over!' Jenny grabbed Pearl's arm and steered her out of harm's way. 'And what are we having afterwards?'

'Can I make some chocolate buns this time, Jenny?'

'Of course you can! And shall I make a trifle again?'

'Mmm!' Pearl nodded energetically. Jenny's trifles were really something – ever so creamy and fruity, with just a little hint of sherry...

Pearl skipped round the supermarket behind a very large trolley.

'Oh, look – crisps – shall we have crisps as well? And Twiglets – Amber loves Twiglets!'

'OK – fine – only *slow down*! You nearly had that stack of baked beans over!'

Pearl giggled, and let Jenny take the trolley. She went off into a little dream...

For several weeks the visit to Mum had hung over her like a dark shadow. She kept turning over and over in her mind what had happened that terrifying day. And the bad dreams kept coming back too. At school she hadn't been able to concentrate, and her work had gone slowly downhill. Mrs Parsons had had a chat with Jenny, and afterwards she had been really kind and understanding, and said Pearl must do what she could, and mustn't worry.

Grace had been marvellous, too. Pearl told her something of what had happened on the visit to see Mum – but not everything. She just couldn't tell her the whole story. That was something private. And Grace had stuck by her at school, and invited her round to tea, and made her laugh when she felt sad.

But one thing shone in her mind like a candle in the dark. She knew now what she wanted. One day, she would go and live with Amber and Tiggy. Back home. On the boat. Where she belonged

Because now she understood. Her mum had sent her a long letter saying how sorry she was, and how she had never meant to hurt her. And Pearl had sent her a *Get Well* card, saying it was OK and she still loved her.

Now Pearl understood two things: yes, her mum really did love her.

And no, she could never go back and live with her.

She knew she needed to live somewhere safe, where she could grow up without being afraid. Where *she* didn't have to be the grown up any more.

Then one day, maybe, when she was much older…

One day, maybe…

And one lovely spring morning, full of daffodils and sunshine, Bernie had come tripping up the garden path, her face one big smile, and told Pearl that Amber had been given permission to visit. Pearl's heart had leapt for joy, and the sad, empty feeling she had had since the hospital visit began to melt away.

Amber was coming to see her!

Pearl had passed the next week in a ferment of excitement. She thought and thought what she would say to Amber, and what they would do. And she would cook for her – something special.

And finally the day had arrived…

'Right – I think that will do!' Jenny steered the trolley to the check out.

Pearl wanted to run and dance and sing; if only Jenny wasn't so *slow*!

The rest of the morning dragged so that Pearl found it difficult to sit still for a second. She baked a dozen gloriously sticky chocolate buns, and made such a mess that Jenny *almost* got cross. Then the telephone rang. It was Grace.

'Grace says, please may I go round to her house for a while?'

'Sounds like a very good idea to me!' Jenny gave a sigh of relief, and then laughed. 'I'll drop you round as soon as I've finished the trifle.'

Pearl ran up Grace's garden path, and rang the bell.

'Come on in!' smiled Mrs Joseph. 'Grace has got something to show you…she's been jumping around like a jelly on springs all morning!'

'Come on up, Pearl!' Grace's beaming face appeared over the bannisters. 'Come and see what I've got in my room!'

Pearl forgot to say goodbye to Jenny and bounded up the stairs.

In Grace's bedroom was a Playstation dance mat.

'Wow, Grace! When did you get it?'

'My gran bought it for me – for doing well at school. It's brill, Pearl – you just put in the disc, and then all these arrows light up on the mat, and tell you where to put your feet.'

Grace switched on the Playstation. All over the big mat there were arrows that flashed on and off to guide your feet.

'Go on – have a go.'

'No – you go first,' said Pearl shyly.

So Grace turned up the music, and leaped onto the dance mat.

Away she went, spinning and turning to the music.

'It's a bit hard at first, until you get used to it,' she panted.

Then she jumped off the dance mat, and fell backwards onto her bed. 'Go on – you have a go now, Pearl!'

Pearl stepped nervously onto the mat. But the arrows were much too quick for her, and she kept falling over her feet.

Grace fell off the bed laughing.

But then suddenly, Pearl got it, and began to dance really well. Faster and faster she bopped, until in the end she fell onto the bed beside Grace.

'It's the best thing ever!' she gasped.

Pearl and Grace boogied all morning, until Mrs Joseph called upstairs to say the ornaments on the piano were beginning to shake.

'Come on down and have some lunch,' she shouted. 'Jenny says you can stay, Pearl, if you like!'

Pearl did like. Mrs Joseph was a very good cook!

She had made them a stack of pancakes; pancakes with cream cheese, pancakes with lemon, pancakes with jam...

'All that dancing has given you a good appetite,

Pearl,' she laughed, as Pearl ate her way through four pancakes.

'That was *seriously* bad, Mrs Joseph,' said Pearl with a sigh of satisfaction. She saw the look on Mrs Joseph's face, and put her hands over her mouth and blushed. 'Seriously bad means very, very *good*,' she explained.

Mrs Josephs smiled and shook her head, and they all laughed.

Pearl made up her mind to ask Jenny to teach her how to make pancakes, so that she could surprise Amber one day...

Then suddenly Jenny was knocking on the door, and it was time to go home.

Pearl spent the early afternoon setting the table, and arranging everything just so. Jenny let her pick some daffodils from the garden, and make a little table decoration, with sprigs from the fir tree and a few cones. It looked really good. Every few minutes she looked at the clock.

Would four o'clock *never* arrive?

She went into the back garden to practise a few hand stands, then she bounced a ball against the wall and hit the kitchen window by mistake.

'Oh Pearl!' said Jenny in her exasperated voice. Then she laughed, and said, 'Look it's half past three. Why don't you go upstairs and get changed?'

Half past three! Pearl dashed upstairs. On her bed,

neatly ironed, were the jeans and T-shirt that Amber had bought her.

How had Jenny guessed that was what she wanted to wear?

She washed her hands and face and slipped into her clean clothes. Then she spent a long time in front of the mirror, trying to fix the beautiful copper and emerald extensions in her hair.

'Not bad,' said Pearl out loud. She gave a last twiddle to a bit of hair that wouldn't behave, and then the door bell rang. Pearl leaped to her feet, and dashed down the stairs.

'You answer the door, chick,' called Jenny.

Pearl flung open the front door.

And there was Amber, all in her best clothes, smiling that lovely wide smile.

She was even more beautiful than Pearl remembered.

For a few tiny seconds Pearl froze with shyness, and then Amber held out her arms, and Pearl rushed into them and hugged and hugged her.

'Bring Amber in, Pearl,' called Jenny. 'It's cold out there.'

Pearl led her friend into the living room. Suddenly she was tongue-tied again.

'I'm so pleased you could come,' said Jenny. 'Pearl has been so excited. Did you have a good journey?'

'Oh you know – the usual story – delays for repairs on the line, and so on,' said Amber.

'How about a nice cup of tea?' said Jenny. 'I'll leave you

182

two in peace for a while, so you can have a good chat.'

She disappeared into the kitchen.

'I've got something to show you,' Amber rummaged around in her bag. She pulled out two big packets of photographs. 'Tiggy says she's very sorry she can't come and see you, so she's sent you some exclusive photos instead!'

Pearl laughed – and suddenly, everything was all right. She looked through the photos.

There was a whole pack of Tiggy: Tiggy in her basket; Tiggy sitting by the stove with her eyes shut, and a blissful smile; Tiggy lying on her back, with her back legs akimbo, and that silly look on her face; Tiggy playing with the Tiggy Teaser; Tiggy standing on her head in the waste-paper basket…

And so it went on.

'They're yours to keep, sweetheart,' said Amber.

'Oh Amber, that's the best present you could ever give me.' Pearl felt tears of happiness in her eyes.

Then Jenny came in with the tea and some chocolate biscuits, and while they munched, Amber showed them both the other photographs.

'Oh – the Christmas photos!' cried Pearl. 'I'd forgotten about those!' And there she was, opening her Christmas presents, her hair all glamorous, and there was the Christmas tree, and Amber in a silly hat eating Christmas dinner.

Jenny was fascinated by the glimpses of the boat. 'I never knew a canal boat could be so lovely inside,' she said. 'And so comfortable, too!'

'Oh you should just see my little cabin,' said Pearl eagerly, 'and the peacock cushions, and stained glass rainbow Mum did on the window...'

Her voice trailed off. Somehow she couldn't think of rainbows just yet. It was much too painful.

'Why don't you show Amber all the lovely paintings *you've* been doing?' said Jenny.

So Pearl fetched the big case Jenny had given her so she could keep her paintings safe, and shyly showed them to Amber.

'That's Grace, my best friend,'

'It's a lovely portrait,' said Amber. 'You've really captured what she's like – I can see she's kind, and funny, too.'

'That's right!' Pearl was surprised.

Then Amber looked silently through the other paintings.

There was one of Tiggy, sitting on top of the boat next to a pot of marigolds. There was one of the boat, sailing along through the meadows. It was winter, and the trees were glittering with frost. Red-berried holly shone in the hedgerows, and in the distance you could see a lock, and a little bridge.

'I tried to remember what it was like just before Christmas,' said Pearl shyly.

There was a picture of the Christmas tree, with all its glittering lights, and one of Amber, steering the boat.

'You've got me to the life there, girl!' laughed Amber.

Then Pearl showed Amber her favourite picture.

Against a bright blue sky, an elderberry tree tossed its creamy little pancakes in the wind. Butterflies danced in a cloudless sky, and on the blossoms tiny bees and hoverflies feasted on the sweet nectar.

Underneath Pearl had written:

The Magic Elderberry Tree.

'Do you know, you can practically *smell* those blossoms!' said Amber. 'I think that's your best picture ever, Pearl. And you've made it *look* magical, too.'

Pearl nodded. 'Oh it is, Amber, it really is. You can feel the magic – sort of all around it…and then, it's such a *useful* tree, too. You can make a lovely drink from the flowers – elderflower champagne – it's ever so easy to make! Me and Mum used to make gallons – only you have to be careful when you take the cork out, because it's really fizzy, and it can explode! And it tastes – oh, it tastes wonderful – of roses and summer, and honey…' Pearl sighed at the memory.

'One day, Pearl, you'll have to show me how,' said Amber gently.

"Course I will,' said Pearl. 'And I'll show you how to make elderberry cordial, too, if…if…'

Amber took her hand silently.

'She really does have a talent for art, doesn't she?' said Jenny.

Amber nodded. 'One day, I'd love to teach her.' She smiled right into Pearl's eyes, and Pearl felt her heart skip a beat.

The time sped by, and soon it was time for Pearl to start preparations for tea. She had planned to cook sausages, bacon, eggs and tomatoes – just as she had on the boat.

'Do you want any help?' called Jenny.

'No thanks – I'm going to do it all by myself!'

Carefully Pearl put the sausages on to grill, while she sprayed a little oil in the frying pan. When the sausages were nearly done, she got the bacon sizzling, and later added the eggs and tomatoes.

She put the plates to warm, checked the table for the umpteenth time, and made a big pot of tea.

Then she stuck her head round the living-room door. 'Tea is now served,' she announced, with a mock bow.

Jenny helped her dish up, and before long they were all sitting down at the table.

'Isn't she a fabulous cook!' said Amber, tucking into her sausages.

'The greatest,' smiled Jenny.

All in all tea was a most successful meal.

'These buns are yummy!' Amber munched away appreciatively. 'Really rich and chocolatey,'

'That's good!' said Pearl cheerfully. 'Only I dropped one of the eggs on the floor – but I scooped it up before Jenny saw, and it mixed in OK.'

Amber stopped mid-bite, and then she and Jenny exploded with laughter.

'Now she tells us,' howled Amber, spluttering with chocolate bun and laughter.

'You're a caution, Pearl, a real caution!' said Jenny, wiping tears from her eyes.

And Pearl blushed, not sure whether she'd been very clever or not.

After tea, Jenny insisted that she would do all the washing up so that Pearl and Amber could have a good long talk. Pearl thought she saw a nod, and a little smile pass between them.

'I'm so full, I shall sink the boat tonight!' said Amber. 'Come and sit by me for a moment, Pearl.' She patted the sofa gently.

Pearl sat down next to her.

'I've got some good news for you, sweetheart.' She took Pearl's hands into her own. 'Social Services have said you can come and stay on the boat with me for a week, and if everything works out, I can be your long-term foster mother. Then, eventually, we can be a Forever Family, you, me, and Tiggy...if that's what you would like...'

Chapter 22

One lovely summer's day, when the sky was as blue as a butterfly's wing, and the scent of clover melted over the fields like honey, a brightly painted narrow boat glided along the Grand Union Canal. Painted on the bow was a golden blossom tree dancing in the wind.

On the roof of the boat, comfortably coiled in a pot of marigolds, a little tortoiseshell and white cat dreamed of fat sleek mice and bacon sandwiches. Inside the boat, two people sat at the breakfast table making plans.

'Six Scotch pancakes this morning,' said Amber. 'You really have recovered your appetite, haven't you!'

'Uh huh.' Pearl swept up the last traces of pancake and honey with her fingers, and licked them dreamily. 'How long will it take us to get to Broughton do you think, Amber?'

'If we make good time, we should be there by tea

time, I reckon.' Amber laughed. 'You're always in such a hurry, girl!'

It was two months since Amber had told Pearl the wonderful news that she had been approved as her long term foster mother, and that eventually, if all went well, she, Amber and Tiggy, would become a Forever Family. Pearl had lived up in the clouds since then, so full of happiness she thought she would burst.

And then in June came a half term holiday, and Bernie said that Pearl could spend it with Amber on the boat, to see how they got on.

'As if I need to find out how we get on!' said Pearl, snuggling up to Amber.

Amber put her arm round Pearl, and gave her a little squeeze.

'There's just one thing, though,' said Pearl slowly. 'You know I really, really want to live here always, with you and Tiggy…but…but I shall miss Grace, Amber. She's the only real friend I've ever had. And I shall miss Willowbrook, as well.'

'I know, sweetheart – and I've been talking about that to Bernie. And I think we've come up with the perfect solution. There's a marina on the Grand Union about three miles south of Granby. We could live there in term time, so you could still go to school at Willowbrook, and see Grace every day.

'And then, in the holidays, we can cut loose, and travel the canals as free as the ducks!'

'Oh Amber!' Pearl leapt to her feet and jumped up and down. 'That's perfect – really perfect!'

'And of course, Grace can come to tea, sometimes, and even for little holidays with us, if her mum and dad will let her.'

Pearl did a handstand, and fell into the waste paper basket.

'That is, if there's any boat left when you've finished wrecking it!' laughed Amber.

'*And* I can still go and see Jenny, sometimes.' Pearl picked herself up off the floor and turned the waste paper basket the right way round again. 'I shall always love Jenny, you know. She was so good to me.'

Pearl went to her cabin, and lifted a large scrap book from her bedside table. She took it into the saloon, to share it with Amber.

It was her Life Story book.

She turned to the last page but one. It showed a picture of Jenny, with her arm round Pearl. Pearl was smiling happily at the camera.

'Bernie took it last week,' said Pearl. 'She said the book's mine, now.'

Pearl turned to the last page. From the very last photograph, Amber and Pearl beamed at the camera. They were sitting on the deck of the boat, and

Tiggy was on Pearl's lap.

'It was good of Bernie to take that yesterday,' said Amber. 'It's our first real family photo, isn't it?'

Pearl nodded. 'It's turned out really well, hasn't it – 'specially of you and Tiggy.'

'It's a lovely one of you too, sweetheart – but the main thing is, we're all together.'

Pearl nodded, happily. A sudden wind blew the curtains, and fluttered the pages of the book. 'How dark it's gone!' she said.

Outside deep purple clouds had smothered the sun. The irises on the canal banks bent double in the squall. Heavy rain drops drummed the roof.

'Going to be a real summer storm,' said Amber. 'We'd better stay put till it blows over.'

Rain slammed against the windows, rocking the boat in the wind.

There was a frantic scratching at the saloon door.

'Oh, poor Tiggy!' cried Pearl. She opened the door hastily. The gale swirled round the saloon, banging doors and rattling windows.

Tiggy shook her hind legs daintily, and sneezed.

'Come on, Tigs!' Pearl took a paper towel, and mopped Tiggy's back. 'She just can't *stand* rain on her fur!'

Tiggy warmed herself on Pearl's lap, and for a while she and Amber watched the storm through the window.

Then, as suddenly as it had come, the wind dropped, and the sun came out.

Amber peered outside. A fine veil of rain slanted against the purple sky, silver needles in the sudden sun.

Then Pearl saw it. 'Oh look, Amber, look! A rainbow!'

Before Amber could stop her she had darted up on to the deck.

Over the dark gold fields, and over the stormy clouds a glowing arc spanned heaven and earth. Pearl felt Amber's arm round her shoulder, as they gazed at the rainbow in silence, oblivious to the soaking rain.

They stood and stared until the rainbow vanished, and sunshine glazed the decks with gold.

'Look! We're steaming!' Pearl felt the hot sun soaking through her wet clothes.

'Come on below, and get changed,' said Amber. 'I don't want you catching cold!'

Pearl threw off her wet clothes, and towelled herself dry. She felt glowing all over, inside and out. In the saloon, Amber was drying her hair. 'What is it about rainbows?' she said. 'Don't they just fill you up with happiness?'

Pearl nodded. But troublesome thoughts crowded into her mind. She tried to push them away, but they wouldn't go. A dark cloud settled on her mind.

'What is it, sweetheart? Can you tell me?' Amber took her hand gently.

Pearl gave a shuddering sigh. 'It's…it's rainbows and

Mum...you know how she is about rainbows.' Pearl nodded her head to the stained glass rainbow on the window. 'She's crazy about them, Amber. She embroidered them on all my clothes when I was little...she said we were the rainbow people...and then, when I went to see her, it was the rainbow on the lid of the jewellery box I gave her that started her off again. And it was...it was the rainbow box that she threw at me, and cut my arm. And you should have seen her room Amber. There were rainbows *everywhere*.'

Amber sat in silence. She held Pearl's hand and gave it a little squeeze to show she was listening.

'And somehow, after that, I've never felt sure about rainbows...'

Amber nodded slowly, and gave Pearl's hand another squeeze.

'And – and there's something else, too. When I was little, she told me the Noah's Ark story, and said it was all about promises...' Pearl took a deep breath. 'There's something I've never told you – or anyone. You know the day the social workers came and...and took me away from Mum?'

Amber gave Pearl's hand another little squeeze.

'Well, I never told you, but the day before that, Mum had been really, really ill...and she drank lots and lots of cider to try and cheer herself up...only it didn't work...she just got sicker and sicker. And then...and then she went on the deck, and started shouting and singing. And people came and stared, and some laughed…and then she got angry, and…and she missed her footing when she tried to get out onto the bank to shut them up…and she fell in the water…'

Pearl took a deep breath. 'And I tried to get her out, Amber. I tried so hard, only I couldn't…she was too heavy—' Suddenly her body was racked with hard dry sobs.

Amber put her arms round her and held her tight. 'Oh Pearl,' she said. 'Oh Pearl.' And she held Pearl while she cried herself out.

Eventually, Pearl continued, 'A man from one of the other boats pulled her from the canal, and a lady came and helped her get changed…and then the lady took me onto her boat, and gave me a cup of tea…and she phoned the police…and then social workers came, and they…they took me away…and I yelled and screamed, but no one took any notice. And when they were carrying me off, Mum shouted, "I'll come and get you Pearly, I promise. I'll come and get you."

'But she never did, Amber, she never did…and that still hurts.'

'It was a promise she couldn't keep, sweetheart. Not because she didn't love you, but because she's too sick.'

Pearl sighed deeply. 'I know that now, Amber…and

194

I understand. But I've been feeling funny about rainbows ever since…and I wasn't sure whether I wanted them all over the boat, either—'

'And yet – you rushed outside to see one – we both did, didn't we?'

'Because they're magic, aren't they? Pure magic—'

'There's a saying about rainbows, Pearl,' said Amber slowly. '"It takes both rain and sunshine to make a rainbow." Have you ever heard that?'

Pearl shook her head. 'Rain and sunshine,' she murmured. 'Rain and sunshine…that's so *true*, Amber. I've never thought of that. Rain *and* sunshine—'

'You know, I think it's the rain and the sunshine in our lives that makes things beautiful,' said Amber.

Pearl thought. She thought of the sunshine days – the safe, blissful days when she was a very little girl, when she had been so happy with her mother…and then she thought of the rain days, when she had ended up in foster care, desperate for her mother, so lonely and sad, and bewildered. And the sunshine days again…Amber, and Tiggy and Grace, and Jenny, and Willowbrook.

'I want to do something,' she said suddenly to Amber. 'I want to write something.'

Pearl went into her cabin and seized her notebook. First she drew a rainbow, and wrote down the names of all the colours. Then she scribbled and scribbled, and crossed out, and sighed, and scribbled again. She worked all morning, while Amber steered the boat steadily on its way to Broughton.

At last with a sigh of satisfaction, Pearl took the poem to show Amber. 'I've written something for you,' she said shyly.

Amber moored the boat in the shade of a willow tree, and took the little note book.

> RED is warm like fire,
>> Makes me think of home and love,
>> But sometimes can be angry.
>
> ORANGE is for joy,
>> And juiciness and laughter.
>> Orange is for fun.
>
> YELLOW is sunshine,
>> Buttercups and Easter chicks,
>> Yellow makes me tingle.
>
> GREEN is for spring,
>> And everything new,
>> For happy beginnings.
>
> BLUE is butterflies,
>> And deep summer skies.
>> Blue is for peace.

INDIGO's dark, like a rainy day,
When the world's full of shadows
That won't go away.

VIOLET is true
And heaven and always
Violet is love.

Amber read Pearl's poem in silence. Then she turned towards her. 'That is a truly beautiful poem, Pearl.' She sat in silence and read it again.

'I wanted to paint it all, but I couldn't think how,' said Pearl. 'I could only say it in words.'

'Hmm.' Amber rubbed her nose thoughtfully. Suddenly she leaped to her feet. 'Got it!' she said. She went into her cabin and ferreted about.

'Have a look at this, Pearl.' She showed Pearl a book with a beautiful cover. It showed a cherry blossom tree against a blue sky. From the branches of the tree, streamed little silk flags.

Pearl traced the picture with her fingers, copying the flow and flutter of the flags. 'That's so beautiful, Amber. But what are all the flags for?'

'Well, in some countries, when people want to make a special prayer, they copy the prayer onto a strip of silk, and tie it onto a tree, so that the prayer can blow all the way to heaven.'

'Oh!' It was a new and wonderful idea. 'So I could do that with my poems! Oh yes, Amber, yes!'

Pearl leaped over the side of the boat, and did three perfect cartwheels for sheer joy. 'What can I write them on, though? I don't suppose you have any silk—?'

'No, probably not – but I've got all sorts of bits and pieces of fabric in my collage bag.'

Pearl's eyes sparkled. If there was one thing she loved, it was rummaging about in a ragbag. She clambered eagerly back onto the boat.

Amber's ragbag was a treasure trove…bits of glittery brocade, old cut up saris, pieces of lace, felt scraps, cotton squares, there were even a few scraps of silk…

'I've got the most brilliant idea, Amber!' cried Pearl. 'I could write each bit of the poem on its own colour – like red on a bit of red material, blue on blue, and so on!'

'Fabulous!' said Amber. She gave Pearl a sharp pair of scissors, and a special pen that wrote on fabric. 'Have fun!'

For the rest of the morning Pearl snipped and wrote. It was quite difficult writing on some fabrics – especially the scraps of silk, but by lunch time she had a neat stack of rainbow flags. Each flag was triangular, and tapered to a fine point at the end.

'So it will flutter really well,' she explained to Amber.

'Are you going to put them all round the boat?' asked

Amber. 'They would wave in the wind most beautifully as we sail along.'

Pearl shook her head.

'NO – I've got a much better idea,' she said mysteriously. And no matter how many times Amber asked her, she kept her secret.

It was five o'clock in the afternoon when they sailed into Broughton Marina. Pearl re-lived all she had felt when she was last there – all that hope, and then the bitter disappointment. Through the marina they chugged, and way down the canal.

And there she was.

The magic elderflower tree, heavy with bees and creamy blossoms.

Pearl leaped out onto the bank before the boat had quite stopped, and buried her face in the blossoms. It was heaven, pure heaven.

Then she took her little rainbow flags, and one by one she tied them to the branches of the tree.

All the colours of her life waved in the wind.

That night, Pearl lay warm and safe in her cabin bed. She drew back the bluebird curtains. A moth burred softly against her window, and found its way inside. It was a pale and delicate green, with silver wings. Pearl shooed it out again, fearing it would harm itself against the light. Then she switched off her bedside lamp and gazed through the window.

Seven flags gleamed softly in the moonlight, all her sorrows and joys blowing in the wind.

She shut her eyes and held Tiggy close. Underneath her the boat rocked gently. In the next room, Amber was singing softly to herself, and through the open window drifted the sweet scent of elderflowers.

Pearl slept.

Turn the page to see some
more Orchard Books you might enjoy...

Do Not READ This Book

As revealed only to Pat Moon

978 1 84121 435

£4.99

WARNING!

Snoopers watch out!
Fierce guard-bunny on patrol!
So paws off this book!
That includes my friend, Cassie. And
especially MUM. Who's FAR too busy
drooling over creepy-crawly Action Man
to care about what I think anyway.

Shortlisted for the Sheffield Children's Book Award

PAT MOON

*Loads of secret stuff about BOYS, worry bugs,
babies, enemies, etcetera, etcetera.
Snoopers will be savaged by Twinkle
(warrior-princess guinea pig).*

978 1 84121 456 6

£4.99

EMILY SMITH

Jeff really liked television. Cartoons were more interesting than life. Sit-coms were funnier than life. And in life you never got to watch someone trying to ride a bike over an open sewer. Sometimes at night Jeff even dreamed television. Mum complained, but it didn't make any difference. Jeff didn't take any notice of her, which was a mistake.

A very funny and thought-provoking book from Emily Smith, winner of two Smarties Prizes.

Utterly Me, Clarice Bean

By Lauren Child

978 1 84362 304 5
£4.99 (utterly worth it)

This is me, Clarice Bean.
Mrs Wilberton, my teacher, wants us to do
a book project – which sounds utterly dreary...
until I find out there is an actual prize. Me and
my utterly best friend, Betty Moody, really want to
win...but how?

'An utterly fantastic book.' The Sunday Times

'Very entertaining.' The Independent

'Feisty and free-wheeling. Hilarious and
irresistible.' The Financial Times

Orchard Red Apples

Utterly Me, Clarice Bean	Lauren Child	978 1 84362 304 5
Clarice Bean Spells Trouble	Lauren Child	978 1 84362 858 3
The Truth Cookie	Fiona Dunbar	978 1 84362 549 0*
Cupid Cakes	Fiona Dunbar	978 1 84362 688 6*
Chocolate Wishes	Fiona Dunbar	978 1 84362 689 3*
The Truth about Josie Green	Belinda Hollyer	978 1 84362 885 9
Hothouse Flower	Rose Impey	978 1 84616 215 2
Snakes' Elbows	Deirdre Madden	978 1 84362 640 4
43 Bin Street	Livi Michael	978 1 84362 725 8
Seventeen Times as High as the Moon	Livi Michael	978 1 84362 726 5
Do Not Read This Book	Pat Moon	978 1 84121 435 1
Do Not Read Any Further	Pat Moon	978 1 84121 456 6
Do Not Read – Or Else	Pat Moon	978 1 84616 082 0

All priced at £4.99 except those marked * which are £5.99